Barbara Greenwood

◆

A QUESTION of LOYALTY

**cover by
Greg Ruhl**

Scholastic Canada Ltd.

Toronto New York London Auckland Sydney
Mexico City New Delhi Hong Kong Buenos Aires

Scholastic Canada Ltd.
604 King Street West, Toronto, Ontario M5V 1E1, Canada

Scholastic Inc.
557 Broadway, New York, NY 10012, USA

Scholastic Australia Pty Limited
PO Box 579, Gosford, NSW 2250, Australia

Scholastic New Zealand Limited
Private Bag 94407, Greenmount, Auckland, New Zealand

Scholastic Children's Books
Euston House, 24 Eversholt Street
London NW1 1DB, UK

Canadian Cataloguing in Publication Data

Greenwood, Barbara, 1940-
  A question of loyalty

ISBN 0-590-71450-3

I. Title

PS8563.R43Q4 1984   jC813'.54   C84-098852-4
PZ7.G74Qu 1984

ISBN-10 0-590-71450-3 / ISBN-13 978-0-590-71450-1

*For Bob, with love and thanks
for encouraging my writing
and correcting my spelling*

Contents

1
Pursued

Dan woke with a start. Something had touched him—something sharp, prickly on his cheek. He opened his eyes. For a second he could see nothing. A dark haze hung over him and the scent of evergreen was everywhere. Then he remembered. Last night he had rolled under a spruce tree for warmth, for protection, for concealment.

His body came slowly to life. He could identify each separate part by the aches: the dull throbbing of his feet, the angry twitches of his leg muscles, the sharp contractions of his empty stomach, the scratchiness of his parched throat, and—almost blocking out the rest—the fire that consumed his left arm. Pray God the wound was not infected, he thought. At least it had been properly bound up the first night.

How long ago was that? His tired brain struggled backwards. Part of yesterday on his own, the day before that with Matthew, the day before that—what?

1

His eyes closed. The pain receded. No . . . Up . . . Must get up . . . They'll find me here. His mind lurched awake again. Three days since the wound had been tended. It should be healing, not burning like this. Water . . . Must get some water. Fire from his stomach was coming up to meet fire in his arm.

Every muscle screamed as he edged himself out from under the earth-sweeping branches. Rolling onto his knees, he used his right hand to push himself up, stumbled onto his reluctant legs, then shakily stood. Dried needles clung everywhere, making him look like a scarecrow trembling in the light December breeze.

Dan steadied himself against a young tree for a few minutes, shivering. As the blood began to quicken in his veins his head cleared, the trembling all but stopped. What time was it? He squinted up at the pale winter sun. Noon? No, later. The sun was too low in the sky for noon. How long had he slept? he wondered. He'd tramped through the night until the river had stopped him. Frustrated and in pain, he'd been too tired to try to find a way across in the dark. The last thing he remembered was crawling under the evergreen. Now it was past noon.

He had to go on. There was no hope of food. The little food they'd been given three days ago had been eaten long before they'd been forced to separate to confuse the militiamen pursuing them. More than twenty-four hours since he'd eaten, then. No wonder he was weak, he thought.

But that was no excuse. He'd gone without food before. The secret, his mother had always said, was to tighten your belt and think of other things. Like getting away. Like escaping.

Something to drink, then he must get on. He felt an almost paralyzing reluctance to leave the cover of the tiny woodlot he was in. On either side stretched open fields through which the half-frozen river struggled. He could get a drink from the river. There were no houses in sight. No one would see him.

He felt as though he were taking his courage in both hands and holding it in front of him like a talisman as he stepped clear of the enfolding trees. Once he was out in the open, once that first step was taken, his wild heartbeats calmed and he was ready to hobble toward the river, alert for any movement but not furtive, not cringing like a criminal. Though now that he came to think of it, he supposed that's what the militia, the dragoons, considered him—a criminal to be hunted down like an animal.

Matthew would have said *they* were the criminals—the authorities, the government land agents —stealing farms from honest folk. Where was Matthew now? If only they hadn't been forced to separate. If only—

Forget that, Dan told himself fiercely. Concentrate on getting away.

The river was steeply banked at this point. The scramble down the slope through waist-high stalks of dead weeds jarred his arm and made the wound burn again. Thank goodness it had been a mild winter. Only the edges of the river were crusted with ice. Down the centre the cold, black water ran freely. By lying on his front and lapping like a dog he could ease his parched tongue. It was not enough. He hitched himself forward with his right arm and plunged his whole face in, numbing his cheeks, shocking his brain completely awake. The icy water eased his throat but made his stomach burn even more.

Enough. He must get on. Stumbling to his feet again, he used his sleeve to wipe his face, then tucked his left hand inside the flap of his jacket and rested his wrist where the jacket buttoned up. The hardtwist, still sturdy three years after his mother had used it to anchor the button on the homespun jacket, supported his arm and eased the pain so he could concentrate all his efforts on getting away.

His mind was clear enough now for him to take his bearings. The river, running through a deep gully, seemed to be coming from the escarpment. Before they'd split up, he and Matthew had been following a road along the escarpment's base. "Keep the escarpment to your right," Matthew had told him, "and it will lead you straight to Queenston. The faster we get there, the better our chances of escape. They can't warn everyone at once. We have to slip through the holes in their net, and the longer it takes us, the more tightly they'll have drawn the string." Ironically, it had been shortly after that that they'd walked smack into a band of militiamen.

"Separate!" Matthew had hissed, and Dan had plunged into the thicket beside the road, concerned only about leaving the sounds of pursuit behind. The woods had been too thick for men on horseback, but had offered no difficulty to the tracking dogs. Dan shivered involuntarily as he heard again the shrill yapping that had seemed to be forever at his heels. Forget that. Forget yesterday. Only today was important until he was safe.

Where was he? He'd gone left from the road, away from the escarpment, and come upon this stream. Four Mile Creek it must be. That was the next one Matthew had said they would have to worry about. How lucky he'd been that Matthew had arrived in time to find him at that disastrous rout on Yonge Street.

"It's the States for us, my lad," he'd growled as the bullets had whizzed over their heads.

For a second before he'd followed Matthew into the shelter of the trees, Dan had looked back. His compatriots, farmers mostly, humble folk, had thrown down their ancient muskets, pikes, pitchforks—whatever they had hoped to fight with—on the frozen, rutted track, and were fleeing north over the fields or back up Yonge Street. Some hardier ones were still fighting—hand-to-hand now—with the militia that had marched out from Toronto. From one side a field piece manned by someone in uniform lobbed

5

grapeshot impartially at defenders and attackers alike.

Where was Mackenzie? Where was Van Egmond? The Patriots had been deserted by their leaders and now there was no choice but to run like whipped dogs. Anger and humiliation burned in Dan's throat. Then Matthew had tugged urgently at his sleeve.

"There's no time to look back now, Dan. Come on."

Dan had turned to follow but not soon enough. He heard a whine like an angry hornet, felt a jolt, then a wild stinging in his upper arm.

"Get down," Matthew rasped. "They've planted riflemen in those trees, the bastards! Keep your head down and follow me."

So Dan had followed. That first night they'd had Matthew's horse. Even carrying double, it had taken them all the way to Dundas before it had gone lame. Matthew had left it with a farmer he knew, in exchange for food and a safe place to catch a few hours' sleep. Then they were off again on foot, with Matthew leading. He knew everything, Matthew did: how to get them across the marsh at Burlington, what rivers they had to look out for. He even knew where a small boat was cached along the shore of the Niagara if taking the ferry from Queenston proved too dangerous. And it was Matthew who had turned this dash for the border into an adventure. Now it had become mere plodding necessity.

With an effort Dan dragged his mind back to the present. Must keep alert...Informers everywhere...Insane to stand here daydreaming like this. He realized he'd been leaning against the stout trunk of one of the alders that fringed the river. If only his arm would stop aching, maybe his mind would work again. No use wishing; he'd just have to make his mind work.

Matthew had said all these rivers flowed north to Lake Ontario. So if he followed this river upstream it should bring him back to the road they'd been following along the base of the escarpment. Sooner or later he'd have to cross, but the river looked deep and swift here. Further upstream it should narrow and he might find logs and stones to help him cross. Yes, that's what he'd do. Walk back upstream using the river gully to hide himself from prying eyes.

He started to trudge along the river's edge. The crackle and crunch of thin ice under his boots seemed to reverberate off the sides of the gully. He felt as though his footfalls were booming his presence to the countryside. A shift up the side of the bank, to where soft snow on weeds muffled the sound, made walking so awkward that he couldn't stride out and cover ground quickly. To one side a branch snapped in the cold. His heart pounded in his throat. A quail erupted in a puff of feathers by his feet and he jumped for cover behind the nearest bush.

This was ridiculous. There was no need to feel

such alarm. Surely anyone seeing him would assume him to be just exactly what he had been—a farm labourer sent out to underbrush the woodlot. Only by rights he wasn't a farm labourer; by rights he should be heir with Matthew to a nice snug little farm.

If everything had gone the way Mackenzie had promised the Patriots, they'd be in Toronto now, telling Lieutenant-Governor Bond Head to his face what was what. But things hadn't gone as they should have, and Dan knew that anyone out scouting the countryside today wouldn't give him the benefit of the doubt. They'd shoot him on sight. If it turned out later that they'd made a mistake—well, hard times make hard men. He had no business lurking in gullies, they'd say.

He must get across this river. There was no point in going all the way back to the escarpment. He could cut kitty-corner from here and meet up with the road closer to Queenston. If only he were as lucky as they'd been yesterday, finding those logs just upstream from the bridge. He and Matthew had just ducked into a thicket while they discussed the advisability of chancing the bridge across Twelve Mile Creek when a troop of dragoons came clattering across it, plumes on their green shakos dancing, carbines at the ready. After that they hadn't dared attempt the bridge, not knowing what might greet them on the other side. So Matthew had led them upstream, and chanced on logs laid across a narrowing in the channel. There had seemed no end to Matthew's luck—yesterday.

So far the gully of this river had been too deep for anyone to make a cattle-crossing, and he'd come across no storm-felled trees. Just then he came to the end of a long sweeping curve. Here the gully widened, and interlaced branches of alders gave way to cold, grey winter skies. Dan could see, a short hike upstream, a log bridge spanning the creek from bank to bank. Maybe a touch of Matthew's luck *had* come with him after all.

For the last half-mile he'd been steeling himself to wade the creek. It looked as though it would soak him only to the knees at this point and there was hardly any ice—no reason why he couldn't clamber up the other side. Even with only one good arm he should be able to hoist himself with the aid of some of the branches that trailed down to the water's edge. But somehow he just couldn't make himself take the plunge, so he'd trudged on, hoping something would turn up. And here it was. Not even a big bridge across a main road, by the looks of it.

A well-travelled road would have given him pause, but this was only a dirt track with a corduroy bridge—logs laid across a framework, no railings, no covering, just an elevated ford some farmer had put up to make a back road passable for his wagons. And the best part was, he could see both ends. There would be no nasty surprises at the far end when he crossed. The dirt track ran through cleared fields on his side of the river, and he could see down the length of it as it wound into woodland on the other side. Past the bridge the gully narrowed again and the creek was lost in a tangle of swamp willow and thorn bushes. Lucky he didn't have to follow it any farther. It was cross here or never, by the looks of things.

Crooking his right arm around a sturdy tree trunk, Dan heaved himself up the slippery slope. The bare soil was already frozen, making it impossible for him to kick footholds in the bank. Where there was grass a thin covering of snow made it treacherous. He pushed against the trunk with his right hand, flung himself over the lip of the embankment and sprawled panting in the snow.

He lay still for a few moments, listening. At first he could hear only the pounding of his own heart. Then it calmed and there was stillness. He pulled himself into a crouch behind some bushes, raised his head and peered cautiously around. The road was still empty, the fields free of any moving creature. It was little more than mid-afternoon now. If he risked the bridge he could be in Queenston by nightfall, perhaps even out of the country. It would be foolish to waste precious hours while the net grew tighter as Bond Head's couriers spread the news around the countryside. Proclamations offering rewards for the capture of any rebel were already appearing on church doors. Soon the whole countryside would be up in arms. Yes, he'd risk the bridge.

He stood and was pleased to find he felt none the worse for his scramble up the slope. His earlier dizziness had disappeared and the pain in his arm had subsided to a dull ache. Squaring his shoulders, he strode toward the road.

The little bridge was sturdily built. It didn't even creak as he stepped onto it. Now that he was out in the open, committed to crossing, it suddenly seemed endless, an enormous span rather than the ten yards it probably was. Once in the middle he would be trapped, unable to dodge to either side as he had done off the road yesterday.

These fancies were foolish. He must be feverish from the wound to be so skittish. Get across, for goodness sake! There was cover on the other side. It wouldn't· take a minute and he'd be able to dive into those bushes. He forced himself to walk with seeming nonchalance so that anyone seeing him from a distance would take him for a normal traveller.

Halfway. More than halfway. Slowly he let out the breath that had been locked tightly in his chest. Three-quarters of the way. Almost there. Suddenly a piercing whistle shattered his thoughts. Instinctively he froze, his eyes searching for the danger. It erupted from the tangle of bushes at the far end of the bridge—a great bull of a boy yelling like a banshee.

"Yeeeehoooo! I got one. I got me a rebel!"

As Dan backed away his mind registered the square head, the little eyes gleaming triumphantly, the massive shoulders. There was no time to turn and run.

His attacker lunged. Dan ducked sideways, under and away from the reaching hands, but the youth wheeled and charged again. Dan spun round to face him. Now *he* was the one closest to the end of the bridge. If he could keep his opponent occupied while he backed off the bridge, he could run for it. He danced sideways as a huge fist flashed past him. The bigger boy staggered, grunting, nearly overbalanced by his own momentum, then recovered to charge again. He was swinging wildly now, Dan thought, fury unleashed by frustration. "Once they've lost their temper," he remembered Matthew telling him, "they've lost the fight."

Dan backed away from the flailing fists. Then, just as the youth made a jump for him, he suddenly stepped forward, one hand flat against the other's advancing shoulder while his heel hooked neatly around his opponent's ankle. Caught unawares, the boy staggered back heavily to the edge of the bridge, teetered on the brink, then slowly overbalanced and crashed into the icy river six feet below.

Gasping for breath, Dan stared at the figure sprawled in the freezing slush below him, but as the boy sat up, shaking his head dazedly, he turned and ran off the bridge and plunged into the woods that edged the road.

As he ran, hunched over to avoid low branches, he was dimly aware of shouted curses. Please, God, let the bridge supports be coated with ice. Make the banks slippery. Don't let him get out yet. Don't let him get out yet! Over and over the words panted through his brain as he ran and ran, afraid if he stopped he would never be able to start again, afraid he might hear sounds of pursuit.

The grey December light filtering through the trees darkened. Dan ran more and more slowly until, dazed and exhausted, he stumbled out of the woods into a clearing. Leaning against a tree for support, he looked around. Where was he? He had no idea which direction he'd run. A short distance ahead of him were farm buildings, a barn and sheds. There would be animals, straw, warmth. By the looks of the sun it was now late afternoon. In an hour or so the farmer would come out to do the milking. Then no one would come near the barn until morning.

He couldn't sleep out again tonight. He just couldn't. He'd have to risk it. As soon as it was dark he'd climb into the hay mow and sleep warm. The decision seemed to soothe the turmoil in his mind. Stiffly he lowered himself to the ground and leaned back against a tree trunk. An hour, at most two, and he'd be warm. His eyes closed.

2
Hide!

Snow was sifting softly through the chill morning air as Deborah trudged out to the barn for the early milking. The empty bucket dragged her arm down. Full, she could scarcely manage it. Milking was really her brother Nat's chore.

"Time he was back here doing his share of the work," Deborah muttered crossly. Then guilt pricked her and she murmured a small prayer for his "safe deliverance."

Every morning and every evening for the last six days, since the night Silas Hawkes had come tearing down their farm lane calling the militia to arms, Deborah and her mother had prayed on their knees, with their hands folded on the family Bible, for what the minister had called at Sunday service "the safe deliverance of our menfolk from the rebel hordes menacing Toronto." The unaccustomed ritual of daily prayers in itself would have impressed Deborah with the danger of the situation, but added to that was the information her best friend, Isabella Crankshaw, had whispered to her in church.

"Mother says they're monsters," Isabella had mouthed under cover of a hymn. "With pikes for spitting women and children like pigs at a slaughter." And she had rolled her eyes to emphasize the horror.

Deborah, who always made allowances for the exaggeration of her friend's remarks, had shivered. She could remember Nat talking at the supper table one night about some gossip he'd heard, news that farmers were forging pikes out by Lloydtown. Her father had frowned. "They're rabid for Mackenzie up there," he'd said grimly. "He's a rabble-rouser, that man. We'll see the countryside up in arms if we don't stop him."

Deborah shivered again, remembering, then quickened her steps as she heard urgent lowing. By the time the warm, sweet air of the barn enveloped her, she had forgotten all but the need to relieve Hezekiah of her burdensome load of milk. There was just enough grey morning light for her to see the reproachful eyes turned on her as she set up the stool and placed the bucket.

"There, Hezzie, Hezzie," she crooned over and over as she milked, her head firmly butted into the cow's side, for Hezekiah was known to be crotchety. If she didn't like the milker, she would crowd closer and closer until her unfortunate victim was tipped backwards off the stool. Then stool and bucket would have to be moved and the whole business would start again, until the clever Hezekiah had backed the milker right up against a wall. Deborah had learned that if she pushed back, she could often get more than half the milking done before Hezekiah crowded her off the stool.

This morning, Deborah realized, there had been hardly any resistance to the firm butt she had given the cow's side. Hezekiah seemed restless and, once some of her uncomfortable burden had been relieved, shifted about and blew through her nostrils in a way quite different from her usual tricks.

"What's wrong, you silly thing?" Deborah scolded. "You're just like the rest of us, I guess. Jumpy as fat on a hot griddle. Mother's been snapping my nose off about nothing ever since Silas Hawkes came riding by with tales of rebels heading this way. What's that?" she squeaked at a sudden rustling. But the barn was silent again. "Rats, Hezzie." She laughed shakily while the thudding of her heart subsided. "I'm just as bad. Scared by nasty old rats." She dragged the bucket free of the cow's nervously shifting feet.

The rustling came again, then a loud sneeze. Deborah jerked up, terrified, to see the hay explode into the rafters above the loft. A body rolled out of the loft and hit the wooden floor with a reverberating thud. Deborah started to scream but the cow, moving suddenly in surprise, knocked her into the grain bin. She lay still for a second, paralyzed with fear, but when the figure started to move she rolled quickly out of the bin and scrambled for the door.

The door was beyond the dark form crouched on the floor, shaking its head as though dazed.

She made a sudden dart, but as she passed the huddled shape, hands reached out and clutched at her long woollen skirts. She gathered breath to scream but the figure was up and a hand was over her mouth.

"Please. *Please*." The whisper was urgent, desperate. "I won't hurt you. Please." Deborah could feel great sobbing breaths as she was pulled back against her captor.

"Deborah. Deborah!"

Her mother's call brought her to life. She struggled against the imprisoning arms which tightened fiercely against her twisting body, then abruptly loosened. She staggered in surprise, but instead of running, turned to stare at the figure which had sagged against a barn support. In the gloom she could see only the silhouette of his face. A straight nose. Eyes so deep-set they were like black coals in this light. A chin that would be prominent when time had tightened the soft, boyish skin. Hair, robbed of colour in the half-light, in wild disarray and threaded through with straw.

He's no older than Nat, Deborah thought, and every trace of fear vanished so that she was able to say in a perfectly normal voice, "Whatever are you doing in our barn?"

"Sleeping." His voice was sullen, resigned. "It's cold in the woods. I've slept out two nights. When I saw your barn I knew there'd be lots of hay. I just had to risk it."

Deborah stared at him, unwilling to believe. "Then you *are* a rebel." She turned to run.

He put out an arm to stop her. "Please listen," he begged.

The earnest voice and young face reminded her that this was someone, after all, no older than her brother. Her fear receded, to be replaced by pity as she felt his hand tremble.

"I'm trying to get to Queenston, to the river. But I can't go any farther without food." His voice broke but his hands tightened on her arms as he said, "Please, some food."

Deborah felt sick with pity. "There's milk," she whispered.

With a low gasp the boy was on his knees, lifting the heavy bucket to his lips. As she watched him greedily gulping the warm milk she thought of those two nights in the woods and shivered. Even here at Queenston, where there were many farms, they sometimes heard wolves howling on a winter night.

He put down the bucket, panting with the exertion of drinking so quickly. In the dim light she could see a gleam of white around his mouth where milk clung to hairs too fine, as yet, to form a beard. Then she saw the bucket, half empty, and quailed at the thought of the explanations to come.

"Deborah Elizabeth!"

"Coming!" She grabbed the bucket, then paused, unsure what to do next. Run and get her mother, she supposed, but he looked so tired and defeated crouching there on the floor that she still hesitated. "You don't seem— You don't seem—" The word "monster" struck her as preposterous as she looked into his weary eyes. "Well, we were told the rebels were . . . fierce."

"So we are." His head came up defiantly and he answered through clenched teeth. "Fierce, and determined to have our rights."

"Rights?" Deborah felt lost. "What rights?"

"Land." He all but spat the word at her. "And roads past it. And fair markets for our crops."

"But there's plenty of land."

"For the likes of you maybe, with your fine barn and fields that were cleared before you were born."

Questions tumbled into Deborah's mind but there was no time to ask them. She had to get back to the house. Suddenly she decided what she would do.

"Stay here until dark," she said, ignoring the suspicious look that darkened his eyes. "My father and brother left for Toronto with the militia five days ago. Only my mother and I are here, so you'll be safe until evening. I'll try to bring you some food when I come out later to feed the pigs."

"Why would you do that for me?"

"I don't know," she confessed, confused by what she was sure her parents would call her disloyalty.

"Deborah Elizabeth, you come right now!"

The sharp call fragmented an answer that seemed to be forming a long way back in her mind.

"Hide," she commanded tersely, seizing the rope handle of the bucket. As she hefted the bucket with two hands and swung it out the door ahead of her, she could hear rustling as he burrowed into the hay.

3
Deceit

Deborah hoisted the heavy bucket onto the verandah, then stood running both palms down the rough wool of her skirt to ease the burning from the rope handle. Her mind whirled. What had she done? Only five days ago, when her father and brother had started out for Toronto, she had been ready to shoot any rebel she saw; now she had one hidden in the barn. What was wrong with her? How could she have done it? This very minute her father or brother might lie bleeding to death from a rebel bullet. She conjured up frightful pictures to punish herself: Nat, one of a long line of rebel prisoners shuffling through the snow, prodded on by those vicious Lloydtown pikes; her father, face down in a deserted field, staining the snow red with his life's blood. The pictures faded, to be replaced by the vision of a tired, white face and the remembrance of a hand that had trembled on her arm.

How could this rebellion be his fault? something in her cried. I *will* get him food. I *will* help him.

Abruptly the door was wrenched open. "Deborah, for goodness sake, come in! How can you be so aggravating at a time like this?" A cough interrupted the scolding voice. "Give me that milk. Breakfast has been out and cooling these ten minutes past." Deborah's mother lifted the bucket. "Is this all she gave? Are you sure you milked her dry?"

"Yes, Mother." Under her apron Deborah crossed her fingers. Lie number one, she thought.

"As if we don't have enough trouble!" Her mother bustled off into the pantry, calling over her shoulder, "And loose that dog. Anyone could sneak up on us with the woodlot so close to the barn."

Deborah turned in consternation to the fireplace, where Rufus lay thumping his tail contentedly. Now she knew the reason for the restless barking that had so irritated her mother last night. Rufus had sensed the boy's presence, would have found him long since if he hadn't been chained to keep him from using the paw that had been slashed open on sharp ice yesterday.

"Down, boy," she said automatically as the dog nuzzled up to her. Then louder, "He's still limping, Mother. If we let him out the foot's sure to get infected."

"Your father said—"

"No one will come in daylight with the militia

all over. The paw needs resting," Deborah ended shrilly, while a little voice at the back of her mind totted up lie number two.

"Don't you raise your voice to me, my girl. It's bad enough having your father away and not knowing whether he's dead or alive without you arguing about everything."

Deborah could hear the quiver in her mother's voice and knew she had thumped the milk jug onto the table to cover that sign of weakness. Penitently Deborah sat down. Until that morning she too had shared her mother's desperate concern for Father and Nat sent into the limbo of the rebellion at Toronto.

In the six days since the Lieutenant-Governor's courier had arrived in Queenston calling on all "loyal men and true" to rally to the cause of "Queen and the unity of Empire," those left behind had been tortured with rumours. Isabella had come running, wild-eyed, with the news that four hundred Indians had attacked the inhabitants of Toronto. Another neighbour had whispered in shocked undertones that the city was besieged by sixty thousand men brandishing pikes and the relief force had been massacred on the frozen hills outside the city.

Deborah and her mother were frantic with worry by the time their one piece of concrete news appeared. Yesterday they had found nailed to the church door a proclamation from the Lieutenant-Governor, Sir Francis Bond Head.

REWARD!
One Thousand Pounds
to anyone who will apprehend and deliver
up to justice
WILLIAM LYON MACKENZIE
who is known to have been traitorously in
arms against his
sovereign
GOD SAVE THE QUEEN!

So the battle was over! On the coattails of that relief had come the news that the rebels, desperate men all, were running for the American border, headed straight for Queenston and the Niagara River. Mounted patrols would be placed along the river, the sheriff promised. Isolated farmhouses would have to take care of themselves. Deborah's mother had gone straight home and placed two muskets, a powder horn, and a pouch of bullets to hand on the kitchen table.

Deborah stared at the black shiny barrels as she tried to force down her cold porridge. Both she and her mother were dead shots. The thought of one of those lead balls ripping into the tired, hungry youth in the barn made her gag.

Mistaking the reason for Deborah's distress, her mother snapped, "Well, it wouldn't be so cold if you hadn't taken so long to do a simple job." The sentence ended with a gasp as a cough caught her.

Deborah choked the last soggy lump down and

cleared the table. Nervously, under cover of the clatter of the dishes she was putting into the pantry, she secreted bread and cheese in her apron pocket.

"Come and we'll get the feeding and watering over with." Her mother appeared suddenly at her side, brushing the pocket stuffed with cheese as she reached under the dry sink for the slop bucket.

Deborah flinched sideways as though scalded. "I'll do it. You're coughing a lot today."

With shaking hands she tipped the buttermilk from yesterday's churning over the pot scrapings and peelings that, along with the shorts from the last milling, made up the daily rations for the pigs. Then, grunting with the effort, she heaved the slop bucket to the door.

As she stood pinning her shawl tightly against the biting cold outside, her mother said, "That's much too heavy for you. I'll help."

"No." Deborah snatched at the rope handle. "Stay inside where it's warm."

But her mother insisted. Carrying the bucket between them, they were halfway to the barn when she started coughing again and had to set the bucket down.

"Please go back, Mother. I can manage easily from here."

Finally, reluctantly, her mother turned back. Deborah watched with relief until the door closed behind her, then hefted the bucket up the slope, the cheese in her apron pocket swinging against

her leg with each step, reminding her of her per-
fidy. Lie number three, the relentless voice at the
back of her mind said.

Thumping the bucket down at the door, she
whispered into the gloom, "Where are you?"

Soft animal sounds breathed back at her.

"I'm alone."

The boy materialized from behind a stall. "Did
you bring some food?"

She held out the bread and cheese and he
snatched eagerly at it. Never having been truly
hungry before, and embarrassed by his greed,
Deborah turned away. She covered the noisy
smacking sounds he made with clatter from the
slop bucket. The few pigs left over from the fall
slaughter crowded round as she called "soo-eee,
soo-eee," absorbing her attention for several minutes. When she turned back he was licking his
fingers. At her glance he stopped and rubbed his
hands down his breeches.

"Thank you. Thank you for the food."

Feeling uncomfortable, not knowing how to
ask the questions that buzzed like disturbed bees
through her mind, Deborah backed hesitantly toward the door.

"I have to get some water for Hezzie and the
others."

In front of the barn stood a sweep well. Her
father and Nat had dug it out only two years ago,
lining it with split cedar logs down ten feet so
that even in winter they could get water easily.
Nearby stood a bucket. Deborah tied it to the

long pole that pivoted on a post some five feet from the well. The balancing action of the pole meant that even quite a small person could hoist heavy buckets of water from the deep well.

When she heard the bucket splash into the water, Deborah ran to the end of the pole and leaned on it to make it sweep out of the well and swing the bucket clear. Her fingers, stiff with cold, fumbled with the rope. Suddenly she was anxious to get back to the barn. She knew what question she wanted to ask first.

She lugged the bucket well into the barn before putting it to him. "Why didn't you answer when I called the first time?" When she realized what his silence meant, she said sharply, "I told you I wouldn't betray you."

"This is no game. If they catch me I'll be hanged or transported."

"Then why did you do it?" She set the bucket in front of Hezekiah, who started to lap.

The boy picked up a handful of straw and, with the instincts of the farm-bred, began to rub the cow down.

"Why did you do it?" Deborah insisted.

Without looking up from the cow he was grooming, Dan began to talk. He told her about the farm north of Toronto which his mother and father had cut out of the bush tree by tree, sowing potatoes and wheat between the stumps, barely raising enough each year to pay the mortgage and keep them through the winter.

But each year things had improved a little.

There was a bit more land cleared for crops, a slightly better road hacked through the bush, a grist mill only three miles away instead of the back-breaking twenty of the early years. By the time Dan was old enough to be a real help, it looked as though things would be all right.

Then the luck turned. The price of wheat fell. His mother took the swamp fever and died of it. Two winters ago they had been reduced to eating the peelings from their seed potatoes before spring finally came.

That summer the crop was better than it had ever been. They thought the bad times were over. The mortgage would be paid off at last.

"But when we got to town with all our crops we found Dorland wasn't paying what he'd promised. Oh, it wasn't just us. No one was getting more'n half what he'd been promised. And it wasn't just us lost our farm and years of hard work because of it either." The sinewy hand clenched into a fist and smote the flank he'd been rubbing. Hezekiah blew crossly and stamped.

"What then?" Deborah patted the cow soothingly.

"We hired out." His voice was sharp, defensive. "What else can a dispossessed man do but work for another? But we'd no intention of just sitting back and taking it. At least, I didn't. My brother was back from the Red River settlement by then. He told us about this man, Mackenzie, who was holding meetings around the countryside to explain how the government up in Toronto was robbing farmers. I was all for going to hear him but my father said he'd have no truck with that rabble-rouser. Matthew lost his temper—he and my father were always at loggerheads over something—and shouted that if it were his farm, by God, he'd have the guts to fight for it."

There was a long pause; then, almost in a whisper, Dan continued. "I came near to flooring Matthew that day—to say such a cruel thing to his own father. Still and all, I thought we should do *something*. Losing the farm on top of losing Mother seemed to take all the punch out of my father. So I decided if ever a chance came my way I'd take it." He snatched up another handful of hay and scrubbed vigorously at Hezekiah, a shuttered look on his face as though he was sorry to have said so much.

Deborah gazed at the stern silhouette of his face. She was fascinated by this glimpse into a life so unlike her own. Of course the Wallbridges worked hard. On a farm everyone had to pitch in. But there was never any lack of food and her father would never let anyone take their land away. Never.

Curiosity stirred in her again. "How did you fall in with Mackenzie?"

He looked up and blinked at her as though he'd been in a trance—or back in that old life. Then he shook himself slightly and shrugged.

"A bunch of us were going around from farm to farm helping with the harvesting when Matthew brought word that Mackenzie was in the neighbourhood. It seemed a good chance to learn something. None of the men talked about it much but I noticed that after supper most of them drifted off. By dusk we'd all fetched up at the barn where Mackenzie's rally was to be.

"A funny little man he was, standing on a wagon shouting at us in a Scottish burr so thick I could hardly follow a word at first. And every time he mentioned them—those land agent and government fellas—he'd fling his red wig down and stamp on it. I didn't understand what he was getting at the first time.

"But by the time I'd been to a few more meetings, I saw what Matthew was getting at. It *hadn't* just been bad luck, losing the farm. It was money-grubbing land agents buying up the best land, and double-dealing government agents using public money for their own good instead of building roads and mills. So when Mackenzie called us to fight, I went."

"And now you're on the run."

To soften those harsh words Deborah handed him a dipperful of water she'd saved from the bucket. As Dan drank she tried to sort out the muddled images in her mind. How keenly she felt the loss of that bush farm. She could see them, father and sons, latching for the last time a rough-hewn door and trudging down the dirt path, their few possessions in wooden boxes slung over their shoulders. And in a few minutes she would go back to a comfortable clapboard house to pray with her mother that her father and brother would be delivered from monsters such as this hungry boy.

"What happened to make you run?"

"Not just me!" His sudden fury lashed out at her. Then he calmed. "Not just me. Everyone that wasn't killed. It was a shambles. Only a few hundred of us at first. No proper training. Half of us without guns or without enough shot to make our guns useful. We had a sort of skirmish near the toll-gate on Yonge Street. Then two days later, when more recruits had arrived, we marched on Toronto. All we wanted to do was show the government there were enough of us to demand our rights. Well, we met a column of militia marching out of the city. No more soldiers than we were, most of them. Then we spotted two more columns coming up on either side. Some of our men, with nought but pikes, started fading off into the woods as scouts rode up reporting more militiamen in sight.

"I was marching beside a farmer I knew a bit from seeing him at market. Suddenly he said, 'I've eight children at home and the oldest only ten.' There was a shout to halt and form lines. As I ran to get into position I saw my marching-mate disappear into the bush. There were shots. Our men at the front answered the fire, cannon started lobbing canister at us from the trees and suddenly men were running everywhere. I saw Mackenzie on his little white horse dashing back up Yonge Street, so I knew it was all over.

"In the confusion it was hard to tell who was

wearing the red ribbons the militia had pinned to their shoulders and who wasn't. I was afraid to use my musket for fear of hitting a friend, and I had nothing else to use. It seemed useless to stay and be cut down by the militia. I'd just ducked into the bush when Matthew appeared. He'd been away for a while, I don't know where. He was the one who told me to head for Queenston. We were together most of the way here, but two days ago we were spotted by a militia group and had to separate. I travelled on my own until I was too tired to go any farther. Then I saw your barn."

"But what now? Most of our neighbours feel as my father does. Most are off with the militia."

"Not all."

"Not all," she agreed. Silas Hawkes, the sheriff's deputy, had called out the militia but he hadn't gone with them, nor had his son Jed. Isabella's father, Ezekiel Crankshaw, had also stayed home, as had a handful of others.

"I was told where a boat would be cached," Dan said. "It's only ten minutes across the river to the American side for a strong oarsman, and there's enough of a current so the river doesn't freeze. Once I'm on the river I'll be safe."

"Where's the boat?"

He looked at her warily. She was offended by his mistrust and glared at him across the cow's back. "I only wanted to know if it was possible to get there easily from here."

"I was told that half a mile north of the town there's an outcropping of rock with a solitary pine and bushes on one side. Do you know it?" The last was said sharply as Deborah started in surprise.

"It's just a mile from here. Fifteen minutes across the fields, due east. At the end of a farm lane." Crankshaw's farm lane, she added to herself. "How do you know it'll still be there?"

"I have to take that chance."

"Will you leave before I do the late milking?"

"I don't know. Soon as it's dark enough."

"I'll have to go or Mother will be coming out. I'll try to bring you something else if you're here when I do the milking." She hesitated. "Will you tell me your name?"

"Daniel Peterson."

"Deborah Wallbridge." She smiled sadly. "Good luck, Daniel."

"Thank you, Deborah. Thank you for ... for everything," he ended lamely, looking down at the brown flank he had been absentmindedly grooming all the while.

Deborah grabbed the empty buckets and ran out into the sharp morning air.

4
Discovered

Hour after hour Deborah dragged through the day, fetching wood from the shed and water from the well, chopping vegetables for the stew pot, setting yeast for the bread. Every time they came to the end of one chore her mother found them another. She'd been like that all week—almost as though, Deborah reasoned, she were afraid that if once she stopped, her thoughts would overwhelm her. Deborah had been resentful of her mother's constant pushing, but today she felt that same urgency. Only today, the faster her hands moved, the more slowly seemed to move the hands of their small steeple clock.

Why hadn't she just told him to leave? It would have been enough to promise that she wouldn't mention seeing him. But he'd be captured for sure roaming around in broad daylight. Well, that was his lookout. What about *them* if he was found in their barn? Of course they could say they hadn't known he was there. Surely no one would suspect the Wallbridges of hiding a rebel. But what if someone *did* look? She had a sudden vision of Dan being dragged from their barn, manacled, marched into town. And at the farm? She couldn't imagine what would happen to them if the sheriff found Dan there. A tiny shudder of apprehension ran through Deborah. For her family? For Dan?

Dan. When had she started thinking of him as Dan? A slight flush crept up her cheeks. She kept remembering the warmth of his hands on her arms. Annoyed with herself for feeling things she couldn't explain or understand, Deborah grabbed the bread dough from the wooden box where it had been set to rise and slapped it onto the table. For the next twenty minutes she pounded it vigorously enough to bring a blush to the coolest cheek.

Kneading the bread dough eased her feelings for a while but by late afternoon, when she and her mother had nothing to occupy them but the mindless knitting of boot socks, she was so nervous that she could barely speak civilly. Her mother responded sharply and they were on the verge of a quarrel when Rufus sprang up from his place by the hearth and bounded, yipping, for the door. Deborah dashed to the window. Her father and Nat were plodding up the farm lane.

"They're back, Mother, they're back!" Deborah shrieked, but her mother was already out the door, crying and holding her arms out to husband and son at once.

"Thaddeus, Nat. Thank God, thank God!"

Deborah, following, thought, Thank goodness he's home. He'll know what to do. He'll help. She was already hugging him when the thought struck her that her father might not see the problem of Dan quite the way she saw it.

Like a snuffed candle the joy went out of the homecoming. Why couldn't they have waited one more day? Deborah thought, and then was so shocked at her feelings that she ran ahead into the house to stoke the fire under the stew and put a kettle on to boil, as if to atone to her father and brother for her divided loyalties. Surely, surely Dan would be gone before anyone needed to go out to the barn.

She was drawing ale from the barrel in the pantry when her father came through the door. "That's my girl," he greeted her, reaching for the mug and giving her a tight hug at the same time.

"Sit down, sit down." Mother bustled in, pushing Nat before her. "How cold you feel, my dears. Here's the stew just ready and the bread nicely cooled. You'll need a bite to eat, I'm sure."

For the next while there was silence. Father and son ate voraciously, their spoons scraping on the pewter plates before Deborah had swallowed her first mouthful. Mary Wallbridge fussed from fire to table and back again, pouring, buttering, mopping the melting snow from Nat's hair with her apron, touching her husband each time she passed as though to make sure he were real and there.

Deborah felt her traitorous thoughts steal out to the barn. In an hour, with this cloud cover, it would be dark.

Finally her father pushed his chair away from the table and settled back to warm his feet on the hearth. "What a treat to taste your good thick stew, Mary. If you knew what Nat and I have had to put up with this last week..."

"Well, what, Thad? Tell us. We've been on edge for days not knowing what was going on. Tell us."

"Well, you know we took the steamer from Queenston—Wednesday last, was it? What a state Toronto was in when we arrived! No regulars. Bond Head had packed them all off to Montreal the week before, he was so sure nothing would happen here. Fitzgibbon rallying the militia, pretending it was 1812 all over again. The Lieutenant-Governor countermanding every order the poor man gave. It's as well the rebels were just as disorganized or we'd all have been murdered in our beds. No, no," he added hastily as his wife gasped. "That's an exaggeration. But they'd made no preparations for us. None at all. Here we'd come to rescue them, and to hear the townsfolk hem and haw when we asked for a bite to eat and a bed to sleep in..." Thad shook his head in disgust. "I'd a good mind to leave them to their fate."

"Whatever did you do?" The other side of the story had surprised Deborah out of her preoccupation with Dan.

"Bedded down in churches, some of us. Others in the schools. Even stables. And the food! Wherever we went the commissary seemed to be someplace else, so we had to rely on the householders. What a scanty offering of watery soup, greasy mutton, and hard bread we've been grudged this past week, eh, Nat?"

Mouth stuffed to overflowing, Nat rolled his eyes and nodded agreement.

"My poor dears. How glad I am to have you home."

"What about the battle?" Deborah prompted.

So her father launched into the tale of their march up Yonge Street, a thousand strong by now, dragging two field pieces behind them. Colonel Fitzgibbon and some of the mounted men rode ahead to reconnoitre while Bond Head charged his horse up and down the lines of marching men like a spooked calf.

"Those of us who'd seen army action were in front, so I could see as soon as we came over Gallow's Hill that the rebels had marched out of Montgomery's Tavern where we'd hoped to engage them.

"That rabble-rouser Mackenzie was dashing around on a white horse looking as demented as the Lieutenant-Governor. We halted well back while the field pieces were drawn up and the side columns came round behind the rebels. We all looked a fine mob, I can tell you. Not a proper uniform on either side and only little red ribbons on our side to keep us from shooting our own men.

"Fitzgibbon gave the order to move into position as the field pieces started lobbing canister, and riflemen fired from the woods. It wasn't proper fighting, just one side taking pot shots at the other."

Deborah could hear in her father's voice the scorn of a man who had fought under that distinguished soldier, General Sir Isaac Brock.

Her mind now back on Dan, she got up to clear the table. Nat hadn't finished all the bread he'd cut. As she wrapped the loaf in an old linen towel and carried it to the pantry, she managed to drop the extra pieces into her apron pocket. She also took part of a small cheese wrapped in cloth and tucked it carefully onto the edge of a shelf near the door, where she could reach it easily as she went out.

As she did so she caught sight of her father out of the corner of her eye. What am I doing? she thought in sudden panic. Stealing from my father to give aid to his enemy. What else could Dan be considered, after all? He had fought against the militia. But he had good reasons, she argued with herself. I would have done the same in his place. I'm sure I would.

As she pushed the kettle of washing water over the hottest part of the fire, her father's next sentence broke through her troubled thoughts.

"...disgusted with Sir Francis. As soon as he saw the rebels were in flight, he ordered his soldiers up Yonge Street to burn down the house of any known rebel. Gibson's was first. 'A stern act of vengeance,' Sir Francis said. Murder, I call it. Turning women and children out into the cold with nothing but the clothes on their backs and most of them a mile's walk to the nearest neighbour. Fitzgibbon tried to argue him out of it, but being a good army man he couldn't disobey a direct order. I can't see punishing women and children for the sins of their menfolk."

"What about the men, Father, the rebels. Will they really be hanged?"

"Some. It's treason, after all. Taking arms against a legally-constituted government."

"But if they have real grievances?" Deborah persisted.

Her father glanced at her quizzically. "Aye, well, some do maybe. But is throwing the whole country into turmoil the way to mend things? You don't know what it can be like, you and Nat. How would you like to see all that pork you salted this fall carried off, in the name of the Queen, by a band of scavenging soldiers? Or that haycock you took three days to build, Nat, put to the torch by a few wild-eyed rebs? You think we've had just an exciting few days dashing about the countryside, missing out on all the chores, but you don't know what real war is like.

"Your mother remembers." He smiled ruefully at his wife. "American soldiers tramping down our spring crops, the new barn in flames. No"—he tapped his pipe on the palm of his hand and flicked the dottle into the fire, his voice harsher now—"if hanging a few of them would save just this township from the senseless destruction we saw back in '13, '14, then I say it's time we hanged a few."

Deborah, about to lift the kettle of scalding water off the crane, dropped the padded pot-holder into the fire. It flared briefly, showering her skirt with sparks.

"Get out of the way before you set us all on fire." Nat pushed her aside and, grabbing the washcloth, lifted the kettle free of the flames.

Her father's talk of hanging rebels started Deborah's mind racing. She had to get Dan away fast. As she beat the sparks out with one hand, she reached for the small cheese and tumbled it into her apron pocket with the other.

"Hey, where are you going? I even poured the water into the basin so you wouldn't scald yourself," Nat protested as she rushed past him.

"The milking. It's time for the milking." She pinned her shawl firmly under her chin.

"I'll do the milking. You'll probably spill it all over the barn." He reached for the bucket and tugged.

"No." In the tussle her shawl came loose and fell to the floor.

"For goodness sake, must you two be quarrelling the minute you're in each other's company?"

Ignoring her mother's sharp words, Deborah began to fight in earnest. Nat, although only teasing, was much stronger. The rope handle bit into soft flesh as Deborah tried to twist the bucket away from him. Tears of anger and fright blinded her to all but the blur of her father crossing the room to them.

"Have it then." And Nat let go.

The sudden release overbalanced her and she

fell to the floor, crashing painfully onto the bucket. Slowly she straightened into a sitting position, wondering how to explain such behaviour to her father. Then she saw the cheese where it had come to rest against his stockinged foot.

"Deborah? What is all this about?"

Panic locked her throat. She could only stare at him, mute and miserable.

"That's the first time I've seen you two so anxious to go out and milk." He stooped to pick up the cheese. "What's wrong, Debbie? You look ...strange."

Deborah rolled onto her knees and scrambled up. What can I say? What can I say? she thought frantically. "Nat's too tired," she started hoarsely.

"Nice of you to think of *me* for once," Nat hooted.

But Deborah was aware only of her father still regarding her with a puzzled expression. "Is something wrong out in the barn?"

"No, no!" It came out too emphatically. "Of course not," she said more softly.

Her father looked down at the lump of cheese still in his hand and then back at her. She tried to meet his eyes steadily, but there was nothing she could do to stop the hot blush staining her throat and cheeks.

"Perhaps I'd better check for myself." He turned back to the fire. She watched, almost in a trance, while he pulled on his boots, turned to the table and reached for a musket. "Is there someone in the barn?"

"No."

Her father looked at her searchingly again, then his mouth tightened in a thin, hard line as though he had failed to find in her face confirmation of her words. As he turned toward the door, she ran to block his way. Firmly, with his free arm, he moved her aside, his face harsh, tired. "Nat, stay here with your mother and sister."

Deborah clung to the door frame, tears coursing down her cheeks. "It's not his fault," she cried at the stiff back advancing on the barn. "It's not his fault!"

Her mother had come up behind her and taken her by the shoulders to bring her in out of the cold. Deborah turned to her. "Father couldn't let them hang him?" she implored. Then, seeing the shock and uncertainty in her mother's eyes, she twisted herself free and fled toward the barn.

Her father stood, a black silhouette, in the doorway. She heard the barked order, "Come out!" and arrived in time to see Dan emerge from the shadows into the half-light near the door, arms raised.

"Who are you and what are you doing on my land?"

"Father, let me explain."

She had slipped through the doorway and stood facing him, obviously on Dan's side, painfully aware that for the first time in her life she had dissociated herself from this warm, loving man who had always stood between her and the harsh world that now threatened her. But even more clearly she could envisage Dan standing between two hooded men on the steps of the gibbet that had been erected in front of the new courthouse in London. The horror of that picture concentrated her mind on Dan.

"Let me explain."

Breathlessly she raced through Dan's story: the despair at losing the farm, the anger at the crooked government agents, the hopelessness of one man alone solving the problem, the determination to do something about it.

She ended abruptly, searching her father's face for some sign of sympathy. She saw nothing but an implacable sternness as he looked at Dan.

"Did you take part in the fighting at Toronto?"

"Yes, sir."

"Do you know what will happen if you're taken?"

"Yes, sir. They'll hang me."

"Did you know that before you joined Mackenzie?"

"Yes, sir."

"And are you now prepared to face the consequences of your choice?"

"Father!" Deborah cried, horrified.

"Quiet, girl. This is a fine position you've put me in. If I let him go, I make a mockery out of what I believe to be right for this country. If I don't let him go . . ."

He surveyed the white-faced pair before him.

"Do either of you know what will happen if we are found aiding a rebel?"

"Yes, sir." Dan swallowed painfully. "They'll burn your house and barn."

Deborah gasped. She could almost feel the soldiers' bayonets prodding them out into the stark December night, smell the acrid smoke, hear her mother's wracking cough as they stumbled through the snow-filled woods to a neighbour's. Even when they got there they might be turned away because they were traitors.

Her father looked at her sadly. "You thought it was an adventure, did you?"

"No, Father. I truly wanted to help him. All he wants is what we already have. Why should he be hanged for that?"

There was a long silence. Then, slowly, her father lowered his gun. The stern lines of his face softened. He seemed about to reach out to her when suddenly he stiffened. The sound of hoof-beats rang through the sharp, clear air.

"Both of you, quick. Into that stall. Don't make one sound. I'll deal with this."

As Dan and Deborah ducked into the stall, they heard the creak of leather as riders dismounted.

"Well, Silas," Deborah's father called out, "what brings you out in this cold?"

Deborah barely suppressed a gasp. Silas Hawkes, the sheriff's deputy!

"Duty, Thad, duty. There's some talk rebels have been seen in the district."

"That so? I'd be surprised to see anyone this far south."

"We had a report some strangers were seen crossing your land. You been back long?"

"Long enough."

"I've orders to search anywhere suspicious."

"There's nothing suspicious here, Silas. My dog and I have just been round."

"Orders is orders. Now stand aside."

"Stand aside, is it?" The bark of authority in her father's voice made Deborah tense with expectation.

"Am I not just back from the defence of Toronto, and my son with me, that I should have to prove my loyalty to the likes of you, Silas Hawkes? Get off my land!"

There was silence. Then boots squeaked on the snow and a saddle creaked.

"Your attitude will be noted, Thad." Deborah shivered at the venom in Silas's tone. "The sheriff will hear of this."

The sounds of the horses retreated up the lane but still Deborah did not dare to move.

Then, finally, her father spoke again. "Come out, you two." And Deborah ran gratefully into her father's arms.

"Thank you, thank you," she whispered.

He held her tightly, comfortingly, with his free arm, but his voice, when he spoke, was stern.

"This won't be the end of it, you know. A man like Silas Hawkes won't let it drop. He worries away at things forever. Why are you always so impulsive?" Tears gathered in Deborah's eyes.

"But warm-hearted," her father continued gently. "Maybe, in the end, a warm heart is better than a cool head. I don't know."

He sighed wearily and turned to Dan. "I agree there have been problems. Wrongs, if you will. I don't agree with rebellion to right those wrongs." He paused. "I don't agree, either, with hanging lads."

"We are going back to the house," he continued briskly. "When I return to do the milking, I expect you to be gone."

As Deborah watched, safe in the circle of her father's arms, she sensed tension flowing out of Dan. His grey eyes met hers. The lines creasing his forehead smoothed and a smile flickered briefly on his lips. Then he was looking gratefully at her father.

"Thank you, sir. I—I—" And with a faint sigh, he crumpled in the snow at their feet.

5
Dilemma

"He's wounded, Mary. We'll need hot water and clean rags."

"Thad, what on earth—?"

"Later, Mary. Nat, a little of that whisky—quickly."

As her father laid Dan gently on the wooden settle beside the fire, Deborah snatched up a linen towel and tucked it under his head. He lay crumpled on the wooden bench, open-mouthed, ashen.

"He's not dead, Father?"

Without answering, her father cradled the boy's head in his large hand. "Where's that whiskey, Nat?" He reached for the cup Nat was holding out to him and dribbled a little into the open mouth. Dan sputtered and coughed. His eyes flickered open, startled.

"It's all right, lad. Drink a little of this and you'll feel better."

Deborah knew she should be helping her mother fetch bandages and water, but she felt stubbornly possessive about this boy she had discovered in the barn. She didn't know why she felt this need to stand guard. It was unlikely her family would suddenly turn hostile and throw him out into the December night, but she couldn't tear herself away.

As Dan sipped weakly at the cup Thad Wallbridge held to his lips, Deborah studied him intently. For the first time she noticed a ragged tear in the sleeve of his coat. In the dim light of the barn she had been aware only of the rough dark cloth worn by most labouringmen. Now, by the light of the fire, she could see streaks of dried blood and the bulge of a clumsy bandage.

"Don't worry, lad. You're safe with us," Thad was saying in a soothing voice. Dan's eyes fluttered once more and then closed, the taut lips relaxed. Deborah could see colour in his face now, and his chest rising and falling in a slow, natural rhythm beneath the dingy shirt.

"What does this mean, Thad? Who is he?" Mary Wallbridge bustled back into the room carrying a worn sheet which she handed to Deborah. "For heaven's sake, Deborah, you might at least have pushed the kettle over the fire. We're going to need hot water." She swung the crane over the fire herself as she talked. "Thad, please tell me what's going on."

"He was wounded at Toronto. He's on the run."

"A rebel! I thought when you brought him in he mustn't be. Are you mad? If anyone finds him here—"

49

"I know. I know." Deborah had never seen her father's face look so old, so careworn. "But what could I do?" He put one arm around his wife, who stood rigid, staring at him. "What could I do?" he repeated.

Deborah heard in his voice the same turmoil, the same helplessness she herself had felt earlier.

"There's something else, Mary. Silas Hawkes came by when we were out at the barn." At his wife's gasp he hurried on. "He saw nothing and I've sent him off with a flea in his ear. But we must get this boy fixed up quickly. Please, Mary . . . "

"Yes, Thad. Yes." The rigidity left her body and she reached out briefly to lay her hand comfortingly along her husband's cheek before she turned briskly to the business at hand.

"Deborah, get that sheet ripped up. Nat, you'd better tie Rufus outside the front door—just in case. Now let's get this coat off and see how bad it is."

Deborah realized that she and Nat—even Father—had been waiting tautly to see how her mother would react. Trapped air flowed out of all three in soft sighs as they turned to do her bidding. Deborah sat in the rocking chair near the fire, tearing the sheet into long strips, watching as her father knelt beside the settle. He slipped his hands inside Dan's coat and around his back, then raised the boy while his wife folded the coat back over his shoulder and gingerly tugged the sleeve over the bandage. It was a makeshift affair

—Dan's sleeve torn out of his shirt, wrapped tightly around his arm and fastened with a tiny brooch, a silver oval with a curly design on the front that Deborah couldn't see clearly. Her mother unpinned the brooch and laid it aside before trying to peel back the bandage. Blood had soaked through every layer and dried.

"I'll have to cut it off. Fetch the scissors, Deborah. Some hot water, Nat." They snipped and soaked, Deborah laying on wet pads to soften the crusted blood while her father peeled back the layers as her mother slit them.

As she sponged, Deborah watched Dan. His eyes had remained closed all the while they had been working over him. She wondered if he had fainted from pain, but as her father lifted the bandage clear Dan drew a sharp breath and his eyes flew open. Deborah yearned to smile reassuringly but her face muscles seemed stiff, uncooperative, and her eyes were drawn in horrified fascination to the wound.

It was a shallow red furrow ploughed out of the flesh of his upper arm. Dried blood had formed a scab over most of it but where they had torn the scab in taking the bandage off, dark red blood mixed with pus oozed out. The flesh on either side was streaked red and puffy.

Deborah caught the glance exchanged by her mother and father and interpreted it instantly. She had seen enough gashes and abrasions to know the wound was badly infected. It would take hours of poulticing to draw the infection, and even that might not stop Dan from becoming feverish. In common humanity they couldn't send him out into the December night in such a weakened state. He'd be dead of exposure before morning. But Silas Hawkes was already suspicious. If Dan was found in their house . . .

It's all my fault, she thought as she watched her parents. But what else could I have done? a voice repeated endlessly in her head, echoing her father's earlier words. What else could I have done?

Thad, still on one knee beside Dan, stared at his wife. He was pale but his voice, when he spoke, had the strong, commanding tone Deborah was accustomed to. "There's no reason why anyone should stop by here tonight. We'll put him to bed in the cubbyhole upstairs and try to keep him from turning feverish."

Mary Wallbridge's lips tightened as her husband lifted Dan's limp form, but all she said was, "Deborah, make up a bread poultice while we get him into bed."

The closet under the eaves would be cold and damp. It was used for storage, with the bed only being made up when company overflowed. Deborah thought rebelliously about the warm bedroom tucked off the side of the kitchen, the one used as guest room or sick room under ordinary circumstances. That's where Dan should be, where they could keep him warm and watch him easily, but her common sense told her why he was being bundled upstairs.

At least I can do something about warming the bed, she decided. While her mother hurried off to get clean linen, she gathered the bricks warming on the hearth for their own beds that night and wrapped them in flannel. She gave Nat all four with orders to put them in the bed right now. He looked as though he might protest the commandeering of *his* brick, so she turned her back and began rummaging noisily in the pantry for the makings of a poultice. And then his mother was calling. There was nothing he could do to show his feelings but stomp up the stairs.

By the time Deborah had blended bread and bran and herbs in a small basin and carried it, along with a small kettle of boiling water, upstairs to the back of the house, her mother and father had Dan settled in bed. His clothes were in a heap on the floor. The sleeve of his borrowed nightshirt was rolled up to the shoulder and her mother was swabbing the pus out of the wound with a damp cloth.

"Moisten that poultice, Deborah," she directed. "The sooner we get heat on this, the better." As Deborah mixed, her mother scooped up the hot mash with a clean cloth and clapped it straight onto the wound. Dan flinched and groaned, sweat beaded on his forehead, but his eyes stayed shut. She bound the poultice loosely in place and rolled the sleeve down over it.

"There. That will do for now. The best thing for him is sleep," she said briskly.

But once they were back downstairs Mary

Wallbridge rounded on both husband and daughter. "What is this all about?" she demanded. "Where did that boy come from? What are we to do with him?" Her voice rose sharply.

"Well, Debbie?" Thad's shoulders sagged as he sat down on the settle where Dan had lain. "Tell us."

Deborah's stomach lurched as she stared back at her grim-faced family. Even Nat was glowering. She had assumed somehow, seeing them at work over Dan, that they'd accepted him, agreed with her. About what? Why *had* she hidden him?

She swallowed the lump that rose in her throat. No words would come.

"When did you find him?" her father prodded.

"This morning." It was barely a croak.

"Exactly when and where? Come on, Debbie. We *must* know."

"Well..." Deborah swallowed again and began to set out the events of the morning. As she talked she twisted the corner of her apron into a tight corkscrew.

"Why didn't you tell me?" her mother demanded as she finished.

"I don't know. I thought maybe you'd...shoot him or...send me for the sheriff. He wasn't dangerous. He was just cold and hungry. What difference does one rebel make anyway?" she burst out desperately.

Her father sat up abruptly. "What difference?" he thundered at her. "What difference? You knew what Nat and I were doing. And what about your

54

mother? Did you even stop to think what would happen to her, to this house, if a rebel-hunting mob came out here with torches? You're old enough to know better, Deborah."

"To know *what* better?" she flashed at him. "How to turn another human being out to starve? To give him up to be hanged?"

"Old enough not to endanger your family on a whim."

"It wasn't a whim." Deborah didn't think she could keep the tears back much longer. "And anyway, everyone knows you fought with the militia. How could anyone possibly suspect us?"

As she spoke, Rufus, still tied outside the kitchen door, began to bark frantically.

6
Accused

They froze. Then Deborah's father rose slowly to his feet. Like an old man, she thought guiltily. Like Grandpa just before he died.

"No matter who this is"—his voice sounded harsh, forced—"no matter *who* this is, just carry on normally. We're relaxing after supper and whoever's out there is welcome to join us." The smack of pipe against palm underlined the "welcome."

From outside came the clipclop of hoofbeats, clearly audible now above Rufus's frantic barking. Thad drew the bolt and swung wide the door. A gust of cold air swirled through the room, lifting ashes from the hearth, brightening the fire.

"Hush that dog before he deafens us," Mary Wallbridge said shrilly as a figure pushed into the room. Silas Hawkes.

And behind him, with a stamping of feet and a gruff, "Evening t'ye, Thad. Evening, all," came Alex Hamilton, the sheriff of Niagara.

Alarm rang through Deborah. Her mind

seemed capable of nothing but repeating "the sheriff" over and over until her father's voice drew her attention to a third person hovering in the doorway.

"Come in then, Jed," he said sharply. "Don't dawdle. We need to get this door shut before we heat the whole of outside."

What on earth is *he* doing here? Deborah wondered as Jed Hawkes lumbered in. He was a sullen-faced boy, large-framed, with powerful fists. Despite her alarm over the sheriff's visit, Deborah's mind couldn't help but fly back to the last time she'd seen Jed. Was it just a week ago? Not even a week, really. Yet it seemed like a month since that dreadful fracas Nat and Jed had had on the dock as the militia were boarding the steamer for Toronto.

Just as she remembered that, she caught Jed's eye. He shot a quick glance at the adults clustered near the fireplace, then sidled over to her, grinning.

"Now you'll be sorry. Think yer so smart! See if yer stuck-up pa can save you this time." His voice rose. "*I* know what you've been up to. You've been—"

"Jed!" Silas Hawkes' voice cut in sharply. "You shut your mouth, boy. I'll tell you when to talk."

The sheriff was shaking hands with Deborah's mother. "Evening t'ye, Mary. 'Tis sorry I am to be interrupting your supper."

"We're finished, Alex. It could only be trouble

that brings you out at night like this. Sit down at the table and we'll get you something hot to drink. Deborah, bring some ale while I heat this poker."

Deborah collected four pewter mugs from the china dresser and hurried into the pantry. Nat was there ahead of her. They exchanged frightened glances, afraid to say anything out loud, straining to hear what was being said in the kitchen while they filled the mugs.

"Out again, Silas?" their father was saying drily. "A cold night to be so busy about the countryside."

"When a man has a duty, Thad, he has to do it no matter what the weather."

Pompous old windbag, Deborah thought as the ale frothed over the side of the mug she was filling.

"Jed? Where are you, boy?" the voice continued. "You come right over here. You've important things to say."

Deborah, carrying a full mug of ale, had to stop suddenly as Jed lurched in front of her and plunked himself down on the edge of the raised hearth.

"Clumsy ox," Nat hissed in her ear, flicking a contemptuous look at Jed.

"Shh," Deborah cautioned as they carried the mugs to the table. She set hers in front of the sheriff, who smiled at her.

"Thank'ee, Debbie. We've nae seen much of ye

in the village this winter. Will ye no be coming in to this dancing party my lassies are setting up?"

"Oh, I hope so, Mr. Hamilton." Deborah tried to make her voice sound light and excited. She hoped the hiss of the poker as her mother plunged it into the ale covered what she felt was little more than a croak.

Silas cleared his throat. "About this business, Sheriff."

"Now dinna rush me, man," the sheriff grumbled. "I'm cold clean through tae ma marrow." Leaning back in his chair, he took a long pull at the mulled ale while Silas sat tautly on the edge of his chair, drumming his fingers on the scrubbed table top.

Thad Wallbridge was lighting his pipe again, giving himself time to think, Deborah knew, while he sucked at the long clay stem, trying to make it draw. The two boys were hunkered down on the brick hearth, eyeing each other warily. Deborah fetched the darning basket. Her mother would never let her sit idle no matter what crisis was brewing up around them.

"'Tis sorry we are tae be dropping in just at suppertime," the sheriff was saying again.

"It's no trouble. We're all tidied away. Will you have more ale?"

"Thank'ee, Mary, no. We'll not be keeping ye long." He smiled at her, then turned to her husband. "I've no need to tell ye, Thad, what an uproar's about the countryside. I'd hopes the trouble would be staying up by Toronto, but it looks tae be spreading. I've just had orders straight from Sir Francis tae put guards on the ferries."

"Sheriff," Silas interrupted. He'd been getting more and more fidgety, crossing and uncrossing his black-trousered legs as the sheriff rambled on.

"Will ye just hold yer tongue, Silas? I'd be handling this my way."

"Handling what, Alex?" Thad asked sharply. "I've no wish to rush you but Nat and I have had a tiring week, so if you've business with us I'd be pleased if you got on with it."

"Och, 'tis these damned rebels, begging your pardon, Mary. We ken yon blatherskite Mackenzie's headed this way and some of his scoundrels with him. Now Silas here is insisting one of them was heading across your land."

"And did you arrest him, Silas?" Thad enquired.

"Well, it wasn't me as seen him. But naturally I knew the sheriff would want to investigate. After all, when a man's country is in danger—"

"Aye, just so, just so," Sheriff Hamilton interrupted testily. "Now as I was saying"—he glared at Silas, who slouched back onto his chair—"Silas claims his lad was tangling with a rebel hereabouts. What with orders from the Lieutenant-Governor not tae let anyone slip through our fingers, and all the daft fools in town blethering on about being murdered in their beds, I thought it best tae just come by for a wee look."

"I see," Thad said coolly. He took his pipe out of his mouth and pointed the stem at Jed. "Perhaps we'd better hear what the lad has to say. Then we'll all know what happened."

"That's right. That's right!" Silas was on his feet, beckoning to Jed. "Come over here, my boy," he said as Jed hefted himself off the hearth and came over to the table. "Now you tell us exactly what you saw."

"I tracked a rebel through the woods right the way to this house," Jed recited glibly, as though repeating a lesson.

"Aye? And then?" the sheriff prompted.

Jed looked from the sheriff to his father in bewilderment. "Well, I dunno. The tracks come to an end. He just disappeared."

"In a puff of smoke, I suppose," Nat scoffed from the hearth.

Deborah clenched her teeth on an hysterical giggle as Jed bellowed, "To *this* house, that's where. Right up to this house!"

"Nat, you keep out of this," Thad ordered sharply. "Now, boy"—he turned back to Jed—"this is a serious charge and you'd better know just what you're talking about."

Jed shot an apprehensive glance at his father. Silas jumped to his feet. "*I'll* do the talking here."

"Ye'll sit ye doon and hold yer tongue, man," Alex Hamilton barked. "Need I be reminding ye that *I'm* the sheriff in this township? Now, Jed—"

"Alex," Thad interrupted in his slow, deep voice, "there's something very puzzling about

61

this. We've already had Silas around once today babbling on about rebels. Now if Jed here had just tracked a rebel right to our doorstep—"

"Didn't say doorstep," Jed protested.

"Still... " Thad's raised eyebrows expressed doubt, scepticism. "There seems to have been rather a lot of pointless to-ing and fro-ing this afternoon."

Deborah looked from her father to the Hawkes, father and son. Jed stood hunched over sullenly. Silas sat poker-straight, nostrils flaring, a tiny muscle ticking incessantly in his left cheek. His knuckles showed white where he clutched the pewter mug.

"It was yesterday—late yesterday—when Jed spotted him."

"I see. It took you twenty-four hours to track him two miles?" Again Thad's eyebrows expressed polite astonishment but he said only, "Well, Sheriff, perhaps you'd better get on with the unfolding of this little mystery."

Deborah wanted to shout, "Hurrah for our side." But a sharp intake of breath beside her made her turn to look at her mother. Mary Wall-bridge's face was white and pinched. She'll give us away, Deborah thought, panic fluttering in her stomach. They'll know we have something to hide.

But the sheriff was talking again. "Now then, lad, sit ye doon and tell us again just where ye caught sight of yon rebel."

Jed edged into a chair, then looked at his father.

"Well, go on, boy. Go on! You know what you saw," Silas prompted impatiently.

"It was at the crick," Jed started. "Pa sent me to mind the bridge."

"Which bridge?"

"What?" Jed seemed startled, uncertain.

"Where the back concession crosses Four Mile," Silas snapped.

"Silas, I'll thank ye tae keep out o' this."

"All right, all right. Just get on with it."

The sheriff, visibly swallowing his temper, turned back to Jed. "Now, lad, tell me what ye saw."

"I was in the bushes beside the road. Heard sort of a scuffling sound. Dog, I thought. Too much noise fer anything smaller. Next I hear footsteps on the bridge. I jump out. And there he was—the rebel."

"And how did ye ken he was a rebel?"

"'Cause he tried to run."

"*Anyone* would run with *you* jumping out of the bushes at them," Deborah burst out, then went scarlet as everyone turned to stare at her.

"Aye. Well, forbye the lassie has a point. Then what happened?"

"We fought."

"Ye fought? Did ye no say he was running away?"

"Well, he was tryin' t'get over the bridge."

"Ye mean tae say he ran *at* ye, not *away* from ye?"

"Sort of."

"Sort of? Sort of? Either he did or he didna, lad. Which is it tae be?"

"We fought, I tell you. And then he ran across the bridge and disappeared," Jed finished defiantly.

"There you are, Sheriff," Silas butted in. "There's a murderous rebel on this farm. Do your duty and search—" Silas's unctuous voice broke off as the sheriff's massive hand slammed down on the table.

"Hold yer peace, Silas Hawkes. There's things I'm not understanding here as yet. Isna this a different story from the one that brought me out here?"

"Your duty as a loyal citizen—" Silas's voice rose shrilly.

"'Tis my duty tae find out the truth," the sheriff roared. "And I have nae had it yet. Now, if ye'll not sit quietly I'll be putting ye outside that door tae cool off."

Silas subsided onto his chair, his lips tightened thinly over clenched teeth. The sheriff turned back to Jed.

"Now then, lad," he said in a carefully controlled voice. "Let's just be filling in a few of the blanks in this picture. Ye fought, y'say?"

"Yes, sir."

"And then he ran away?"

"Yes, sir."

"And what might *ye* have been doing while he was running away?"

Jed stared at the floor. Everyone in the room stared at him. Deborah almost felt sorry for him. An interesting speculation was growing in her mind as she visualized that fight — the hulking Jed, the slim and nimble Dan, a slippery bridge . . .

"Well, lad, what were ye about?"

"What does it matter? Get on with the important part. You're wasting time," Silas snapped.

"What does it matter? What does it *matter?* A lad sent out by one of my deputies tae guard a bridge lets a rebel walk across it bold as brass, doesna report it for twenty-four hours, and ye ask me what does it matter?"

"Now look here, Sheriff—" Silas spluttered.

But Jed was on his feet bellowing, "I didn't let him. I didn't let him! I'd of broke his cursed neck fer him if he hadn't of knocked me in the river."

There was a moment of startled silence. Then Deborah could feel the tension in the room slowly dissolve as a picture formed in each mind of the lumpish Jed flat on his back in the freezing slush. But the bubbles of laughter died in Deborah as she looked at Jed. A purple flush stained his face; his hands clenched into fists.

"Laugh at me, will you," he snarled, looking straight at Nat, who sat pop-eyed on the hearth. "Think yer so high and mighty. Yer nothin' but a pack o' traitors." He lunged at Nat but the men had jumped to their feet.

"Silas, see tae yer lad!" the sheriff barked as both he and Thad grabbed Jed's arms.

Jed jerked violently against Thad's restraining hands, but was suddenly and surprisingly quiet when his father barked, "Sit down, Jed! You leave this to me, do you hear?"

As Jed slumped onto his chair, Deborah realized that she and her mother were on their feet, backed into the chimney corner. She felt shaky as she sat down again—and cautious, as though she were in a cage with a wild animal. She looked at Jed, hunched over in his chair, unable to believe how wild-eyed and terrifying he had been for those few minutes.

Of course he'd always been a bully—a sly, behind-the-teacher's-back type of bully. When adults were around he scarcely said a word. It was only smaller or weaker children who knew what a nasty, jeering tongue he had or how sneakily those pudgy hands could dart out to pinch or punch.

There was no punch in him now, Deborah thought. He was staring sullenly at the floor again as his father said, "You've heard the story, Sheriff. My boy tracked the rebel right onto this farm. Let's get busy."

"Now hold hard, Silas. I'm just trying tae figure this out for mysel'. If 'twas *yesterday* all this happened, how is it that you've only just come tae me, and it past suppertime?"

"Well, naturally we didn't want to bring you

out on a wild goose chase, so we tracked the rebel ourselves. Picked up his trail nice and easy in the woods and followed it straight onto this farm."

"And then?" the sheriff prompted.

"And then what?"

"Where exactly did it lead ye—this trail of footprints?"

"Well..." Silas shrugged. "There's new snow about. Besides, it was coming on for dusk."

"Coming on for dusk? What about the rest o' the day, man?" the sheriff roared. He looked from Jed's hangdog face to Silas's furious one.

It was Thad who answered. "I imagine, Alex, that Silas didn't know about Jed's little run-in until late this afternoon. Once he'd wormed it out of the boy, he rode straight here to see what he could find out."

"And was ordered off! A strange way for a loyal citizen to act—ordering a sheriff's deputy off the property," Silas sniffed.

Thad ignored him. "Well, Alex, I've no doubt it all happened just as they said. There's little a man can do, after all, about people crossing his land."

"Aye, well. The times, ye ken. They force us tae do things..." Alex Hamilton looked apologetically from one Wallbridge to another.

"Just so." Thad stood abruptly and laid his pipe on the mantelpiece. "So, now that we've heard the story, shall we have a look in the outbuildings? Rufus and I only got as far as the barn before Silas interrupted us the first time." He was striding to the door as he spoke. Men and boys trailed after him.

"'Twill look better in ma report, d'ye ken?" the sheriff was saying as they all trooped out. Rufus bounded after them just before the door slammed.

Deborah and her mother sat frozen by the fire. Mrs. Wallbridge jerked her needle to and fro in the sock she was darning, so that it became puckered and twisted and useless. Deborah had to lay the darning egg in her lap. Her hands were shaking too hard to hold it. She could not stop thinking about Jed Hawkes.

He'd always held grudges. That look he'd thrown at Nat as the two of them had followed their fathers out the door had been almost triumphant. He couldn't possibly know about Dan. He *couldn't!* Was this all just a plot to get back at them for that scene on the dockside when the men left last Wednesday?

If only she'd kept her mouth shut then. If only she hadn't needled him. "Think before you speak, Deborah," her mother was always saying to her. She hadn't that day.

They'd been up early, she remembered, even though the steamer wasn't leaving until noon and it was less than an hour's ride into Queenston. Her mother had wanted to pack a substantial lunch for her menfolk—who knew when they'd get food next, what with rebels marching on Toronto? Thad and Nat had oiled the muskets. They had already spent most of the previous evening, after Silas had delivered his message, melting lead and pouring it into moulds to replenish their supply of musket balls. Nat had filled several leather pouches—some to take with them, some to leave for his mother and Deborah.

Finally the time had come. They had ridden to town in silence. It wasn't really like going off to war, Deborah remembered thinking, but a musket ball could kill a man just as dead in a skirmish as in a full-scale battle. So they'd all felt tense, and when Jed Hawkes had come swaggering along the wharf and ordered her off the keg where she was sitting to watch the loading of the newly-arrived steamer she'd felt—well, ornery.

"I'll move when I'm good and ready," she'd said, tossing her head defiantly. "Who do you think *you* are, giving orders?"

"Clear out of here, I said." He loomed menacingly, one hand raised as though itching to slap her.

A demon of stubbornness possessed her. "Just get on with your work, Jed Hawkes," she'd said loftily. Hitching the heavy wool shawl more tightly around her shoulders, she'd settled herself firmly on the upturned keg that sat with a dozen others on the dockside, ready to be loaded. "You can have this one when you've done all the rest."

Jed's square face flushed an ugly, mottled red and Deborah's stomach knotted sharply. Trembling with rage, he drew back his hand. Deborah gritted her teeth and tried to stare him down. She would *not* move for the likes of Jed Hawkes.

"Jed! Jed Hawkes!" The shout sliced through the tension. "Keep your hands off my sister!"

For a second Deborah went limp with relief, but Jed had wheeled like an enraged bull, furious at the sudden interruption.

"Look out, Nat!" Deborah screamed, springing up.

Jed, as he turned, snatched up a small keg and hoisted it with both hands over his head, ready to hurl it. Nat dodged sideways. Jed lurched after him, tripped on a coil of rope and crashed full-length on the dock at Nat's feet. The keg burst open, spilling lead musket balls everywhere.

Deborah gasped. "If that had hit Nat ... !" She looked at her brother. He'd gone white around the mouth, but when he caught her eye he grinned cockily and raised his fist in a quick victory sign. Deborah started to giggle.

A knot of interested onlookers had crowded around when the fight started. No one offered to help Jed up. He rolled groggily into a sitting position, blood gushing from his nose.

"What's going on here?" a deep voice demanded, and the little group around Jed parted. Deborah's father stood there, hands on hips.

"Well?"

Deborah swallowed her giggles. "I'm sorry. It was my fault. I made Jed angry."

Thad Wallbridge turned to his son, who said quickly, "He was going to hit her."

Jed, still stunned, was sitting spread-legged on the dock, shaking his head like a great, woolly bear. Thad eyed with distaste the blood smeared over his face and down his coat front. "You'd best cut along home and change, lad. And the next time you're given a job to do, tend to business and never mind about girls."

Snickers from the bystanders had followed Jed as he'd staggered to his feet and slouched away, but Deborah hadn't felt like laughing. She was aware only of the black scowl he'd turned on her as he left.

Was that what this was all about? Getting back at them for that public humiliation? Was his story about a rebel on their land just a shot in the dark or did he really know something? No. Impossible! How could he? But where would they search after the outbuildings?

Suddenly a babble of shouting erupted outside. "Ho, the house! Ho, the house," came a great roar.

Deborah ran to fling the door open. Cold air swirled round her. She could hear the stamping of horses' hooves and a voice bellowing out of the darkness, "Get the sheriff! He's needed at Queenston."

There followed the sound of running footsteps, a low-voiced conference, the jangle of harness, and suddenly the sheriff was mounted and wheeling his horse while Silas and Jed scrambled to follow. Deborah felt her mother come up behind her in the doorway. Together they watched as the riders clattered into the dark of the lane.

It was over. Dan was safe.

7
Interlude

Deborah sat in a circle of sunlight near the attic window, her foot pumping the treadle rhythmically, her fingers feeding wool to the twirling spindle. The weak winter sunlight—warm through the glass—and the humming wheel soothed her soul, freed her mind to drift lazily. She needed this peace after yesterday.

Her mother had sent her up to sit with Dan, but he was sleeping deeply. The fever had broken early that morning, and after a few sips of broth, he had fallen into an exhausted sleep. The narrow cot had been pulled out of the cupboard slightly so that Deborah could keep an eye on him as she sat spinning. She studied him now while her fingers pulled and released, pulled and released the exact amount of fluff needed to twist a strong thread.

His hands, resting on the quilt, were long, thin, large-knuckled, sinewy. Hands that would work neatly, she thought—not clumsy, destructive hands. His face, smoothed of pain lines and vulnerable in sleep, was long, narrow. Surely a sensitive soul lived behind those sharply-etched cheek-bones and sunken eyes.

She knew so little about him, had talked to him for such a short time, and yet in one day he had turned their lives upside down, put them all in danger. She wanted desperately to know that she had been right to hide him, that he was worth the trouble, so she searched his features intently. Then his eyes flickered open and he was staring back.

She started slightly and the thread snarled, knotted and snapped. She lifted a hand to stop the wheel. "How are you feeling now? Would you like something to drink?"

He ran his tongue over parched lips and smiled painfully. She got up quickly.

"I'll moisten this cloth for your lips first. That'll make you feel better." She dipped a linen towel into the jug standing on a low table near the bed, then patted his lips with it. She dipped it again to wipe the rest of his face but he hitched himself up in the bed slightly.

"Thanks. I'll do that." His voice was scratchy.

"Don't knock that arm," she warned as he raised himself on one elbow. His hand shook as he took the cloth, but he seemed determined to do it himself, so Deborah turned back to the jug and poured water into the tin mug. Still on one elbow he took the mug.

"Drink it slowly." But he had already finished and was sinking back on the pillows, his eyes closed. She took the cup from his trembling hand, worried about the effect of cold water on his weakened body, but after a minute his eyes fluttered open again and he smiled.

"Weaker than I thought," he gasped. "Sorry—"

"You just lie quietly. Fevers are weakening. You don't want to undo all our good work." She sat down at the spinning wheel again, and when his eyes closed, reached for the snarl of thread. Breaking it with a deft twist, she backed off the wheel to free more thread, picked up a handful of fluff from the basket of carded wool at her feet, and spliced the two strands together. The wheel had been singing for some minutes when he spoke again.

"What happened last night?"

Deborah's fingers fed the spindle automatically while her mind sorted out last night—what to tell, what was better not told. "You fainted, so we brought you inside and cleaned the wound. Do you remember anything of that?"

"Vaguely. I remember being brought up here and then some kind of commotion. Voices—men's voices quite close."

"That was ... nothing really. Neighbours came round—"

"Angry voices," he insisted.

"There's nothing to worry about," she said firmly, as though willing him to believe her. Then, feeling the thread thicken between her inattentive fingers, she reached up to stop the wheel. "The sheriff was here. My father showed him around and he went away satisfied."

"Showed him around! Why did he come in the first place?" She didn't answer. "If I don't know, I'll fret more than if I do, Deborah," he said gently.

"The man my father ordered off last night dislikes us. He told the sheriff some story about his son seeing you on our land, and made him come out to see."

"His son? A great hulking brute?" And when she nodded, "He saw me all right. But nowhere near here."

"He claims they tracked you here."

Dan sank back on the pillow and closed his eyes. "How could the sheriff not have seen me? Didn't he come upstairs?"

"No. They searched the outbuildings first." She paused, remembering. "I was terrified they *would* come up here. You were well hidden, but if you'd moaned or turned in your sleep . . . "

"I should never have hidden in your barn in the first place. It was selfish. I thought I'd be gone before dawn."

"We could have gotten rid of you easily enough."

"Why didn't you?"

"We've never turned a stranger in need from our door. I didn't think of your family being on one side and mine on the other. You were just a benighted traveller."

"Your mother and father wouldn't see it like that," he said sceptically.

"No." Deborah thought again about last night, then said, "I didn't really understand what I'd done until we were dressing your wound and I saw how upset, how frightened they were. I thought nothing in the world could frighten my father. I've seen him grab the nose-ring of a stampeding bull and turn him single-handed. And yet he was afraid to have you in the house." She realized she was almost pleading with Dan to explain this to her.

He was silent for a moment, then he sighed. "It's easier to be brave when you know what you're doing is right."

"But it wasn't wrong to take you in! They don't think so any more than I do." And when he just looked at her, she continued. "Last night, after Sheriff Hamilton and the Hawkes left, my mother and father were talking. They said . . ." Deborah stopped. She needed to sort out her thoughts. There was an important bit, a comforting bit, and she wanted to offer it to ease the pain she thought she saw in his eyes. She tried again. "They were talking about being on one side or the other. Father said we chose the side we believed in, just as you did. If Mackenzie had won, the boot would be on the other foot. Would you have turned me from your door?" She stopped, satisfied, as a faint smile banished the bleak look from Dan's face.

After a moment he spoke again. "You didn't finish telling me about last night."

"Where were we?"

"I was taking good care not to moan and groan."

His dry tone made her smile. "As it turned out, it didn't matter anyway. I told you I was terrified all the time they were outside that they'd be searching in here next. But suddenly there was a terrific commotion out in the yard. Someone started hallooing for the sheriff. I was never so close to fainting in my life."

"What did they want, whoever arrived? Some poor soul hunted out, was it?"

"No, no. Nothing like that. The steamer had arrived with new orders from Sir Francis and they'd been all over the countryside looking for the sheriff so he could open them. Thank goodness they came when they did. Father said Silas Hawkes was trying to persuade the sheriff to look for footprints by lantern light."

Dan sat up at that and exclaimed, "Footprints! I was so tired that I wasn't at all careful."

Deborah laughed, but seeing Dan's scowl said quickly, "There probably *were* footprints, but it snowed again early this morning. I had a very good plan for getting rid of them, but when I went to look before breakfast there was no trace."

Dan looked bemused. "What were you going to do? Drag branches?"

"I was going to make snow angels all over them. In fact I was going to do it last night. My mother said if anybody saw me it would be a dead giveaway that we had something to hide,

78

but my brother said if anybody saw me lying out in the woods at midnight flailing my arms about, they'd just think we'd been hiding the fact I was loony."

Mary Wallbridge, coming up the stairs to the surprising sound of laughter, said, "That's encouraging! You must be feeling better. I've brought you some nice broth to help you get your strength back."

But Dan lay still in the bed, his grey eyes regarding her intently. "I must thank you, ma'am. I realize—I'm sorry, I know your household is in danger while I'm here. I'm very grateful. I'll leave as soon as—" And he sat up as though to get out of bed.

"You get right back in there and lie still. We've had enough trouble with that fever. Now see what you've done!" Mrs. Wallbridge scolded as Dan fell back, panting. "I appreciate how you feel, but we took you in with our eyes wide open and, to be honest, you'd be more danger to us roaming about the countryside in the state you're in than you are tucked up here in bed. If somebody saw you in a dead faint in a snowbank they'd know for sure you hadn't made it that far under your own steam."

Deborah felt this speech was a little abrupt and unwelcoming. She wanted to soften it with phrases about "doing unto others" and "being not forgetful to entertain strangers," but Dan's grey eyes seemed to be regarding her mother warmly as he sipped the broth she held to his lips.

"That reminds me," Mrs. Wallbridge continued. She fished in her apron pocket. "We found this when we were cleaning your wound." She held out the little silver brooch.

"My mother's," Dan said, making no move to take it. "I had no other way to keep the bandage in place. Matthew has one like it, only his has an S for Sophia, my mother's sister. The C is for Charlotte."

Deborah thought he was rambling, that the fever had returned. He ran his tongue over his lips and took a deep breath as though he was in pain.

"I'd like you to have it, if you would, Mrs. Wallbridge."

"I would be honoured to wear your mother's brooch, Dan, but there's no need—"

"Please. Without your kindness it would be loot for whoever captured me. I'd like to think that no matter what happens to me, you have it safe."

Silently Mary Wallbridge pinned the brooch at the collar of her dress. "Now," she said briskly, "when you're feeling a little stronger you can tell us your plans for getting over to the States and we'll see how we can arrange it. In the meantime, the more sleep you get, the sooner you'll be on your feet."

But Dan seemed unable to sleep. He lay staring at the ceiling long after Mary Wallbridge had gone downstairs. Deborah thumped the treadle and the wheel sang softly in the silence while she sorted out all the questions she longed to ask him.

His mother was dead, but what about his father and brother? She supposed the question of getting safe away was uppermost in his mind, but she wanted to know things that would fill in for her the shadowy outlines of his life: the small farm north of Toronto, the struggle to make it pay, the bitterness when it failed. There must have been more to his life than that—plans, dreams. As she pondered, her fingers automatically fed the wheel and the spindle slowly filled. She had stopped the wheel and was changing the spindle before he spoke again.

"I keep wondering what happened to my brother Matthew."

Deborah looked at him in surprise. "Where is he then?"

"I don't know; we had to separate. If only he got away safely. The whole thing was my fault. I don't know how I'll ever find him again."

"Do you mean he was with you at the battle?"

"Just at the very end, then after. We ran into a band of militiamen and had to separate the day before I fetched up in your barn. He said to head for Queenston, we'd meet up there." Dan stopped, then said bleakly, "But I've been too long about it. If he managed to escape he's disappeared into the States long ago."

His voice was so despairing that Deborah searched her mind for anything that would comfort him. "I'm sure the sheriff would have mentioned last night if anyone had been caught. I don't think a soul has been arrested down here."

Dan was silent for so long that she had leaned forward to see if he'd fallen asleep when he spoke again. "Well, I guess the important thing is to get out of here. If only I didn't feel so weak. Just sitting up makes me dizzy. I must get away."

He seemed to have forgotten Deborah's presence entirely. She felt a stab of resentment and tears pricked behind her eyes. She just managed to stop herself from saying stiffly, "We have every intention of helping you get away." Instead she swallowed the lump in her throat, and knotting the thread around the full spindle, laid it in the basket beside her.

She touched a knuckle to an eye threatening to spill over tears. How stupid you are, she chided herself. Of course he's anxious to get away. And everyone in this house but me will be glad to see the back of him.

She sat up straight, briskly rubbing her hands together to transfer the lambswool oil from the front to the back of them. Since they always spun with the grease still in the wool, Deborah's hands, which might have been red and rough from all the washing she did, were kept soft and white by the lanolin. She looked at them as she fitted another empty spindle in place, then glanced at Dan, but he was still staring at the ceiling. Sighing, she started up the wheel.

"What will you do if the boat isn't there?"

Dan transferred his gaze from the ceiling to

Deborah. He paused just long enough for her to realize that he was still wary about trusting her, then said, "My brother has contacts down here. He told me who to ask."

When he offered no name Deborah tried a different approach. "If you lived up by Toronto, how did he know his way around here so well?"

"He moved around a lot. He's a carpenter. He was going to take me on as an apprentice. Teach me a trade. Farming's too chancy, he said. Well, I guess that dream's gone up in smoke."

Before Deborah could stop herself she said, "But surely he should have started when you were younger. I mean—"

"He's been out west for years, out in the Red River settlement. I hardly knew him when he came back last year."

"He must be a lot older than you."

"Eight years. He was the oldest, then three who died, then me."

That was too common a story for Deborah even to comment. The Wallbridges had their own infant graves in the little cemetery out in the orchard. She went on with her probing. "Your father must have been pleased to see him."

Silence. Finally, "Matthew is a great one for stirring things up. He left in the first place because—well, he was always telling my father he'd been rooked, taking land instead of money." Then, at Deborah's puzzled frown, "My dad was a sergeant in the British Army. Came over during the war—'14, I guess—after they'd done for Napoleon. The regulars were disbanded here, given their choice of back pay in money or land. Dad took land. Trouble was, the best land was saved for the officers. Anyway, Matthew went off ten years ago saying he wasn't going to break his back for a piece of swamp. When he came back and found the roads just as bad and all those acres the church owns still bush, he said right out my dad was crazy. That's when he started taking me off to Mackenzie's meetings. Dad was furious. Thought Matthew was teaching me republican ways. And I guess he was because here I am with nowhere to go but the hated Republic."

Deborah heard bitterness in his voice, felt in him the pain of divided loyalties—the fascinating brother returned from who knows what adventures, the father working long hours to build a farm for his sons. She wasn't sure she liked this brother. All her sympathies were with the father. She felt she had to probe the wound once more. "What is your father doing now?"

He didn't answer, just stared at the ceiling, a muscle twitching in his cheek.

"I'm sorry. I shouldn't have—"

"It doesn't matter. He's working as a hired hand...for a neighbour. The neighbour has"—he paused as though searching for the right word—"influence in Toronto. He now owns our farm."

Deborah said nothing. Because she wanted to know him better she had wrenched out of him all his family's shabby little secrets. Now she felt ashamed, hot with embarrassment. Should she apologize for her nosiness, for what else could it be called?

Her hands, from long training, had never faltered at the wheel, and now a second spindle was full. She reached up to stop the wheel, then took a long breath, meaning to say something to excuse what she now saw as callous prying. But when she looked at him, Dan's eyes were closed and his breathing steady, rhythmic. Just as well perhaps.

She sat quietly, her hands lying idle in her lap, thinking about the next few days. Get him well first, and then what? Crossing the river was so dangerous. There must be another way . . .

A flicker of movement caught her attention and she glanced out the window, then turned to stare intently. Rising quietly, she knelt at the little window to peer through the bubbled, distorting glass. Surely what had caught her eye was a coattail disappearing behind a bush? Someone was skulking about the fringes of the woodlot. There it was again. A bulky figure stealing out of the woods, crouching low to sneak up on the outbuildings. Jed Hawkes!

Thinks he can't be seen from the house, Deborah snorted disdainfully. Then despair washed over her. Was there no hope for Dan? Oh, leave us alone! she cried inside herself. Why can't you leave us in peace?

8
Visitors

They had two days of peace. Then early on Friday morning, while Deborah was washing the breakfast dishes and her mother was putting the last of the bread in to bake, a clatter of wheels sounded out in the yard. Deborah had just dropped the washcloth and was running to the window when the latch rattled and the door flew open.

"May I come in? Pa's putting the wagon in the shed but I hopped out so I'd be first in."

"Isabella!" Deborah cried delightedly as a dark, laughing girl bundled up in a thick plaid shawl bounced into the room.

"Isn't this dreadful, coming so early? But Pa *would* come now and I was determined not to miss a visit. Oh, Mrs. Wallbridge, do you think this is just dreadful of us and you with your baking not finished yet?"

"Don't be foolish, Isabella. You know we're always pleased to see you. How's your mother doing these days?"

"She's some better, thank you. But not enough to be out in the cold. She sends you these." Isabella brought a small linen parcel out of the folds of her shawl, which slid to the floor as she unwrapped two earthenware pots. "Plum and cherry," she said, holding out first one hand and then the other to Mary Wallbridge.

Deborah picked up the discarded shawl, thinking how exciting life seemed with Isabella around. She made the air crackle. Even Mary Wallbridge, who tutted in exasperation about "that silly little girl," smiled when she said it.

"I must send some of my goose grease back with you. That's what your mother needs for that chest of hers. I hope she's keeping herself warm and rested," Deborah's mother said as she scraped vigorously at the kneading board.

"Oh, yes. Katy from down the road comes in mornings to help out, so between us we get all the heavy work done." Deborah knew that for all Isabella's fun-loving ways she worked hard at home. Her mother had been sickly for years, and even though the Crankshaws could afford to hire in kitchen help, it was Isabella who did the managing. "What can I do to help?" she was saying now.

"Just push the kettle over the fire, if you would. The men'll be in shortly, I dare say, and we could all use a cup of tea. Deborah, we'll set out those teacakes I just baked and Isabella's jam."

"I think Pa's come about these rebels," Isabella announced, stripping the linen covers off the jam pots.

Deborah nearly dropped the plate of teacakes. In the excitement of Isabella's arrival she had completely forgotten about Dan sitting in Gran's old rocker by the upstairs window. He had been determined to get out of bed and get his strength back. Thank goodness her mother had insisted he stay upstairs until his legs were less shaky. Surely he must have heard Isabella arrive. Would he know not to move up there, not to walk across the floor?

Deborah's delight in Isabella's visit flickered out. For the first time ever she would have to guard her tongue, not only because Isabella was a chatterbox but also because they didn't quite know where Ezekiel Crankshaw's loyalties lay. He was a forbidding, taciturn man—more so, her mother said, since his son Angus had run away from home all those years ago after a violent quarrel. He had refused to accompany the militia to Toronto but he had also condemned the rebels roundly as misguided fools. Deborah saw her mother's mouth tighten as she moved into the pantry with the last of the baking utensils, and knew she was thinking the same thoughts.

Feet stamping on the verandah brought Deborah out of her reverie. The door swung open and Nat appeared, his arms full of kindling. "Pa and Mr. Crankshaw'll be in directly. How're you, Isabella?" He tramped across the room with the firewood. As he passed the girls he dropped his voice so his mother couldn't hear him. "Still got your baby-fat, I see." He grinned at Isabella.

She flushed red and stuck her tongue out at him.

"Shut up, you pig," Deborah hissed under cover of the wood clattering into the bin. Nat had teased them both from babyhood. In those days he would fling his taunt over his shoulder as he ran from two avenging furies. Now the girls felt too grown up to hit him. He had all but given up on Deborah, who usually ignored him, but Isabella could be most gratifyingly riled. Her eyes were still snapping when Mrs. Wallbridge came out of the pantry.

"Were they on their way in, Nat?"

"Nope. Standing talking up on the threshing floor. Pa sent me on ahead once I'd seen to the horse."

"Well, we'll make the tea now. If it stands too long they'll just have to water it. Deborah, fetch the caddy."

Tea was made and sitting ten minutes before they heard the men on the verandah.

"A good morning to ye, Mrs. Wallbridge."

Ezekiel Crankshaw was a tall, stoop-shouldered man with the narrow, bony face of a Highland Scot. He had lived in their district for twenty-five years, but still couldn't bring himself to be less formal with the neighbour women. Deborah had often wondered if it was because he had started off as a hired hand and then married his employer's daughter. Certainly he'd worked hard enough to rescue farm and mill from the mismanagement of the amiable but drunken army officer who was Isabella's grandfather.

Deborah knew that her father thought highly of Ezekiel Crankshaw, but she had always been afraid of him, terrified both by his shaggy grey hair that stood up in a wind like the ruff on a wolf, and by his harsh, deep voice—even though, as she often complained to her mother, he never growled more than a word to her at a time. Her mother had laughed at her fancies and said no doubt it came of tending sheep all those lonely years in the Highlands before he emigrated, and she should make allowances. Deborah noticed, however, that he had no trouble talking to her father. Indeed, he seemed to be doing all the talking, but broke off abruptly as they stepped into the kitchen.

"Mary, Ezekiel has been telling me some disturbing news. I think we'd better all hear it."

Deborah caught the quick lift of the head and the disapproving look Ezekiel Crankshaw flashed at her father, but Thad said, "The children have to live with this too. They're old enough to share the burden."

He sounded so grim, so solemn, that Deborah's stomach muscles tightened in apprehension. Was it Dan? Had the Hawkes been up to something else? Or had some other catastrophic thing happened as a result of this rebellion? She barely managed to keep her hands steady as she poured the tea. They were all sitting around the table now, her mother saying sensibly, "It'll keep till you've had a cup of tea. You'll be chilled through with standing out there in the barn, even if it has been warmer these last few days."

But her husband had barely downed his first cup before he began. "This rebellion has let loose some ugly feelings about the countryside," he said heavily. "No one seems to have actually caught a rebel on the run yet, but there's a band of young bucks riding about the township harassing anyone who's expressed sympathy with Mackenzie in the past. Tell Mary and the children what you've heard, Zeke."

"Aye. First off I'd better tell them about Mackenzie himself. The word is he got away safe and sound and is fixing to set up headquarters on Navy Island just out in the river here."

"Well," Mary Wallbridge exclaimed, "there's a nerve for you! And what does he hope to achieve by that, pray tell?"

"I've no idea, ma'am. I've just been telling your good man here, the militia's being called out again. At least," he added quickly as he caught Mary's sudden look of apprehension, "MacNab's taken his men from Hamilton down to set up camp at Chippewa, right across the river from Mackenzie. 'Tis rumoured Mackenzie's angling for help from the American government."

The words fell, heavy as stones, into their midst. Everyone in the room knew what that could mean. Even though Deborah, Nat and Isabella had never experienced war, they had heard story after story about the American invasion in 1813. Deborah had often longed to see her father in his red tunic dashing about the countryside on his black gelding, leading charges, repelling the enemy. He had been a lieutenant at the time of the last sweep that had pushed the Americans back into the Niagara, out of the peninsula, and kept Canada loyal to the Crown.

Deborah had been thrilled by his stories, reliving every sensation with him as he told how the gelding had been shot from under him on Lundy's Lane so that he'd had to lead his men on foot, rallying charge after charge until dark came. Soldiers on both sides had crawled, exhausted, from the battlefield. It wasn't an outright victory, but at least the Canadians still held the field. The red tunic worn that day, wrapped in silver paper in her mother's linen chest all the years since, had seemed to Deborah a talisman that called up more exciting days than her own. Now she saw in it the colour of blood—her father's blood, Nat's blood, Dan's blood.

"But I really came to warn you," Ezekiel Crankshaw's deep rumble broke into Deborah's thoughts. He looked quickly at Thad Wallbridge who, teeth clamped around his pipe, nodded his encouragement. "Now, I don't mean to scare you, but you're a wee bit isolated here—" He broke off and looked helplessly at Thad.

Ezekiel Crankshaw saw himself as a shepherd still, and his womenfolk were his sheep. If a wolf was prowling the countryside he felt it his duty to keep his sheep in the fold safe and sound and ignorant. The nasty details were for men. He couldn't understand Thad Wallbridge teaching his wife and daughter to shoot as straight as any man and then letting them roam the countryside. He'd even heard that Deborah rode astride when she was out with her brother checking fences. He'd let his own daughter learn to drive the horse and wagon, but that was as far as he intended going. Leaning his elbows on his knees, he stared down at his large workman's hands and continued.

"Nasty doings we've had about the countryside since Mackenzie stirred these troubles up. I've not seen anything with my own eyes, mind, but it's going about the town that a man up near Burlington had his pea rick torched because he was thought to have hidden Mackenzie, and Owen Evans that was so friendly with Mackenzie all those years ago when the little blatherskite lived in Queenston, he's had his wagon lifted by MacNab's militiamen—for the cause, they told him, to help get things over the portage to Chippewa. More likely because he was thick as thieves with Mackenzie. And"—he broke off again, looked at Thad, then said firmly— "and other things better not mentioned. I just wanted to make sure you were on the lookout. Reputations don't count for much these days. Well, Isabella, we'd best be going." He rose abruptly.

"Oh, Pa, I haven't had time to say two words to Deborah."

"Told you this wasn't a social visit, but you would come."

"Well, couldn't I stay a bit longer? That is, if I'm welcome?" She turned an expectant smile on Mrs. Wallbridge and Deborah, who thought, Dear God, no. What am I to do if she stays? Dan can't even cross over to the bed without the floor creaking. Plans to keep Isabella downstairs and talking while she sent Nat up to warn Dan raced through her head. Suddenly she realized there'd been a long silence and Isabella was staring at them, stricken. She'd asked for politeness' sake, never once doubting her welcome.

"Yes, of course, Isabella," Deborah said too quickly and too brightly.

"Nat can drive you home after dinner," Mary Wallbridge added.

But Isabella, still staring at Deborah while the hurt on her face turned to anger and then hauteur, said, "Oh, I'm always saying things without thinking. I just remembered I promised Ma to come straight back and . . . and finish off the bayberry candles we started yesterday. Thank you so much, Mrs. Wallbridge," she said, not looking again at Deborah, "but I'll come another day and sit with you awhile."

"Isabella, wait!"

But Isabella had thrown her shawl hastily around her shoulders and pushed out the door past her father who, Deborah now realized with a stab of alarm, was watching her own very expressive face intently. She caught his eye and felt

94

warmth reddening her cheeks, but his face remained impassive. His eyes swept on to her mother and caught suddenly on the silver brooch at her throat. Mary Wallbridge, still seated at the table, put a hand up—almost involuntarily, it seemed to Deborah—as though to cover the pin. Her hand hovered in the air, undecided, then reached instead for the empty cups. Distracted, she rose with them in her hands as Ezekiel broke the electric silence.

"Something else I meant to tell you." He turned to Thad. "Don't suppose you'd need some carpentry done? Good man just come to town. Could direct him this way."

"Can't see that we have a need for him just at the moment, Zeke, thanks all the same," Thad said after a moment's hesitation.

"Well, I'll say good-bye then. About what I was saying earlier"—he seemed about to say more, thought again, and ended abruptly—"forewarned is forearmed, I daresay. Morning, Mrs. Wallbridge." He flicked another intense look at Deborah's mother before following his daughter out the door.

"Nat, run ahead and fetch out the horse and wagon, would you?" Deborah's father was saying as he followed Ezekiel Crankshaw out into the chill December wind.

The door thudded shut and mother and daughter were left shivering in the draft until the smell of bread sent them both scurrying to the bake oven let into the brick wall beside the open fire.

"I don't know what's going to come of all this," Mary Wallbridge muttered distractedly as she fished around in the oven with the bread peel. "Oh, will you look at that? The back ones are too brown."

With a thump she slid the cast-iron bread pan off the flat wooden paddle onto the kitchen table, then went back for the next pan while Deborah took a knife and loosened the edges of the loaves already out.

"I cannot figure that man out...Well, the ones from this side aren't so bad," she continued, switching back and forth between the two subjects uppermost in her mind. "I don't think he pays us a visit once in five years and here he is on our doorstep right after breakfast—" She broke off as her husband stamped in.

"Thad, what was Ezekiel doing here? You can't tell me he came just to gossip about Mackenzie."

"No, Mary. What he was too delicate-minded to tell you is that Silas Hawkes has been up to something rather unpleasant."

"What! Whatever do you mean, Thad?"

Her husband sat down heavily, shaking his head. "I don't know what that man thinks he's up to. First he comes haring out here full of accusations, then he goes rampaging off to the Taylor's. He's always been rather officious, but this rebellion seems to have unhinged him."

"Thad, *what* are you talking about?"

"Sorry, Mary. Come and sit down. What Ezekiel came to tell us was that Silas fetched up at the Taylor's yesterday morning. Cal was away to the mill at St. David's, and Silas took to shouting at Betsy. Said Cal was in league with Mackenzie because he attended a few meetings last summer at Lloydtown. Said all the rebels in this township were going to hang and he'd see Cal was first. Well, the long and short of it is that Betsy had hysterics and fainted. She hit her head on the hearth, which started things off early, and she's lost the baby."

Deborah gasped and her mother jumped up. "Oh, Thad, that wicked, wicked man. I must go to Betsy at once."

"It's all right, Mary. Ezekiel said her mother and aunt are both there now."

"But, Father, why did Mr. Crankshaw particularly come to tell *us*?" Even as Deborah asked, the answer began to form in her mind. Somehow Ezekiel Crankshaw knew they had something to hide. He also knew, as did the whole township for that matter, that Silas had an old grudge against her father and Cal Taylor.

She could see Cal Taylor standing in this very room last summer, anger and despair making his voice shake as he explained to her father. "I've tried everything. She pushes through a bush fence. She lifts the rails right off a rail fence. I've even tried lugging stumps over. That only stopped her for a while. And every time I complain to Silas he says it's up to me to make my fences better. He's never blinkered her like you told him and this time she led the whole herd in and they tramped down enough wheat so's I won't be able to make a mortgage payment, and a baby coming and all."

Deborah had been sent out of the room, but she could hear enough to piece together what had happened. It was a common enough problem. Thad Wallbridge, as one of the two township fence-viewers, often had to make a judgement between a man with a breachy cow and a neighbour whose fences wouldn't keep her out. Silas had been ordered to blinker the cow, hang a board over her eyes so she couldn't get a square look at Cal's fence to jump it or push it down and lead the others astray. When he hadn't bothered, Thad had levied a fine which, as official fence-viewer, he was not only empowered to do but obliged to do. Despite that, Silas Hawkes had been furious with both men.

When Silas had wormed out of Jed the story of the rebel on the bridge and they had actually tracked him onto Wallbridge land, Silas must have been overjoyed. The chance of catching the Wallbridges concealing a rebel must have seemed like the perfect revenge.

And he's been balked of it, thought Deborah. That's what's sent him haring over to the Taylors', screaming threats at poor Betsy—mean, paltry spite.

But still, why was Ezekiel Crankshaw in such a lather to tell the Wallbridges about it? As Deborah's mind reached that point again, she heard her mother agreeing with her.

"Yes, Thad, why did he come dashing over here to tell us?"

Her husband sighed and reached for his jar, tamping fresh tobacco into his pipe before he answered. "I don't know what exactly was in his mind, Mary. He's a hard man to read. He's never come out wholeheartedly for either side. Certainly no one could call him a rebel, but he has scant use for MacNab and his ilk in the militia. However, his two messages were very clear. Silas Hawkes is on the rampage and the militia is going to be called out again very soon. I doubt we have anything to fear from Ezekiel, but I do know this —we must get that boy out of this house before Nat and I are called away again."

9
Decisions

Thad had barely finished when they heard floorboards creaking overhead and then the sound of laboured footsteps on the stairs. As they turned to the doorway at the side of the fireplace Dan appeared, trembling with weakness, one hand braced against the wall for support. Even so, his voice was firm.

"If you'll allow me to stay until dark, Mr. Wallbridge, I'll be on my way then."

And when they all stood staring at his rigid white face and purple-smudged eyes, he continued, "It would be better if I stayed in one of the outbuildings. Then if they should come back they couldn't accuse you of harbouring me."

"It would be better," Thad said abruptly, "if you used the sense God gave you. Sit down, boy, before you fall down. How far do you think you'd get in the state you're in now?" And he put his hands on Dan's shoulders.

Under the pressure of Thad's hands Dan collapsed onto the settle by the fire. Deborah could see that he was trembling. Was it from weakness, she wondered, or the effort of steeling himself to make that offer?

"Tell us what plan you had and we'll see what we can do about it," her father prompted. "We're involved now. The faster we can get you across the river, the safer it will be for all of us."

So Dan told her parents the story Deborah had already heard about his brother Matthew and the location of the boat, in a clump of bushes marked by an outcropping of rock and a single pine, on the first farm that ran down to the river north of Queenston.

Everyone in the room but Dan had a clear vision of that spot as he described it. And Deborah knew that the same question was in her parents' minds as hers. Was it with or without Ezekiel Crankshaw's consent that a boat was hidden on his land?

"What I can't figure out is how your brother knows that boat is there. This rebellion sprang up very quickly. No one could have foreseen the need for an escape route."

A crimson flush swept over Dan's pale face at Thad's words. "He's very much a coming-and-going man, is my brother. I mean to say—I don't think it was just for Mackenzie he was roaming about the Niagara Peninsula."

"You mean he was smuggling?"

"He had a lot of money. Not that he flashed it about, but I overheard him insisting that my father let him pay off the mortgage on our farm. I thought he'd made the money out west—he's a dandy carpenter—but my father said he'd not touch a penny of his dirty money. And what with one thing and another, I pieced it together."

"I see. Well, that answers one question in my mind, at any rate. That boat must be there without Zeke's knowledge. There's no way he'd be involved in such a thing."

Deborah saw Dan flush again and felt a sudden rush of anger at her father for using such a contemptuous tone. It wasn't, after all, as though *Dan* was a smuggler! She was about to rush into heated speech when there was a stamping of feet on the verandah and Nat came in.

"Ten full bags and one half one, ready for the morning," he announced, oblivious of the tense silence. "Shall I thresh enough to fill the last bag?"

"No, we'll leave that. I have a more urgent job for you." Thad regarded his son thoughtfully, then said, "There's something I want you to look for."

"Thad, no. We can't involve Nat in this. He's not old enough. He's just a boy."

"Ma!" Nat was protesting in a mortified voice, at the same time as his father said, "We're all involved in this, Mary."

"I'll do it," Deborah butted in. "I know exactly where to look. It's less than an hour there and back." She was stripping off her apron, excitement flooding through her at the thought of action, of doing something worthwhile to help.

"Don't be ridiculous, Deborah," her mother snapped, at the same time as Dan cried, "No!"

"Why not?" She turned furiously on Nat as the safest one to attack. "Anything you can do, I can certainly do."

"It's not that you couldn't do it, Debbie," her father said with a hint of a chuckle in his voice. "It's just that you'd be too conspicuous in your skirts. Nat, with his axe over his shoulder, will just look as though he's out to split some rails."

"What is this thing I'm supposed to do, anyway?" Nat demanded, still standing by the door with his boots on.

"Take your things off, son. We'll have dinner while we discuss it," Thad said.

In the end Deborah spent the afternoon at home churning butter while Nat went out exploring. She sat with the churn between her knees, plunging the dasher up and down. Would the butter never come? Her arms were aching. Her back was sore. Surely it was taking much longer than usual, or did it just seem slow compared to her racing thoughts? What was keeping Nat so long anyway? Maybe he couldn't find the boat. If she'd been allowed to go . . .

On the other hand, maybe it would be better if he didn't find the boat. After all . . . She turned the idea over in her mind again. Well, why not? It might work. She'd ask her father as soon as he came in from loading the wagon. If they had kept Dan hidden this long, there was no reason why they couldn't keep him hidden a bit longer. Then they could just turn him into their hired man. That would be a lot less dangerous than letting him cross the river in his condition—wouldn't it?

"You'll turn that cream sour, scowling at it," a quiet voice interrupted her thoughts.

Deborah looked up. Dan sat surrounded by a snowdrift of goose feathers, the bird between his knees plucked pink and ready for market. When Thad Wallbridge had refused Dan's help in heaving the bags of grain onto the wagon, Dan had insisted on plucking the geese to be sold at the market in the morning. Geese and ducks, along with eggs when the hens were laying and butter when they had nursing cows, Deborah and her mother took to the stores in Queenston as credit against whatever they needed to buy. Few women in the township were as good with geese as Mary Wallbridge, and her birds always fetched a high price. The butter money Deborah was allowed to use for herself.

The paddle was no longer sloshing through the cream. Deborah could hear the soft, sucking *pop* it made when the cream was beginning to thicken, and knew that her tired arms would soon be able to stop, so she smiled at Dan and answered him pertly. "My butter is always sweet."

Dan smiled down at the goose and gave a last tug at a recalcitrant pinfeather. "It was very kind of you to offer to find the boat."

"No, it wasn't kind. It was selfish. I wanted to

do something more exciting than just sitting here churning butter. But now I've got a better idea. If Nat doesn't find that boat—" She stopped when she saw the sudden panic that flashed across his face.

"Don't worry, we'll keep you safe," she said hastily, then stopped again as a frown of annoyance replaced the first look. She remembered her mother saying that invalids tended to be touchy, and wondered how she could explain her plan to him without setting off his prickly temper.

But even while she rehearsed phrases in her mind, his face cleared and he said, "Do you remember the story of Deborah in the Bible?"

"Yes, of course."

"Well, you remind me of her. Intrepid."

"Oh." She thought for a moment. "Is that a compliment?"

"Yes," he said firmly, and smiled at her.

She could feel her face getting warm, and to hide her confusion said, "Oh, the butter. It's ready." And she hurried out to the pantry for the large wooden bowl they used to wash it.

By the time Nat returned, the butter was washed and packed into the butter boxes that printed onto each pound block the long, curly *W* Nat had designed one winter. Deborah had just unmoulded the last brick and wrapped it in linen when they heard the sharp yipping Rufus used to greet one of the family. Mary Wallbridge left the soup she was stirring and peered out the window just to make sure, then pulled the door open. Everyone in the kitchen turned expectantly as Nat came in.

"It's there," he announced. "Found it easy as pie."

Deborah could feel rather than hear sighs of relief from everyone in the room: Dan repairing a cracked chair leg, her father sitting by the fire mending harness, her mother at the door. Only her own wayward spirits fell. Her mind searched rebelliously for some reason why this was not a good idea—his shoulder was too weak to row all that way; there was no way to get the boat back; if her father or Nat went with him, someone might see him. Better to forget about the boat.

"Tell us about it over supper," Mrs. Wallbridge ordered. "Deborah, clear your things off the table, please. The soup's just ready."

As they ate they listened in silence to Nat's story. He had little enough to tell. He'd found the boat easily. The outcropping of rock with a lone pine standing up like a ship's mast was unmistakable. Anyone chancing on the boat would assume a farmer had stashed it there as many farmers along the river did. But Nat had had a good look at it. There was no name written on the stern. Their own boat—impounded by the sheriff a week ago when the troubles broke out, along with all the other boats on the river—was clearly marked *Wallbridge*. Anyway, Nat was positive Ezekiel Crankshaw kept a large boat upriver where there was a better beach.

The trouble with this location was that the boat would first have to be lowered four feet into the water, and then the rower would have to clamber down into it with no way to steady it. And even worse, it was plainly visible from the more accessible riverbank that was now being patrolled constantly.

"If I'd tried to move that boat, they'd have heard me for sure," Nat concluded as he finished the last of his bread. "I don't know what happens at night along that strip, but in the daytime it would be impossible. Especially for one person alone."

The expression on Dan's face darkened as he listened to Nat's words. He sat hunched in his chair, staring at his empty plate, one fist clenching and unclenching nervously on the table.

Thad tilted his chair back and lit his pipe. "Well, tonight's out anyway," he said finally. "The moon's near full and there's no cloud cover. Besides, we'd be better off to find out just what kind of patrol's been posted. It should be easy enough to do that tomorrow. The whole town will be buzzing with news and speculation. No one'll think it odd if I ask the occasional question or two." He sucked again at the pipe, the stem clenched between his teeth, then said, "If we get that boat into the water, could you row it across?"

"Yes, sir." Dan looked up, his face brightening. "My brother said it was only a fifteen-minute row."

Thad tapped his pipe against his teeth thoughtfully. "The current's still running strong. You'll have to pull against it."

"I know I can do it. I'm really quite strong. I've just been dizzy the past few days and that's over now. It'll be a relief to know I'm not a danger to you anymore."

"Speaking of danger," Mary Wallbridge interrupted, "now that it's full dark anyone can see through that window."

Deborah turned in alarm, remembering the glimpse she'd had of Jed Hawkes skulking round their outbuildings the other day.

"Rufus'd bark long before anyone got close enough, Ma," Nat protested.

But Dan said, "You're right. I shouldn't be down here now the daylight's gone." He got up and started for the stairway while Deborah and her mother cleared the table.

"We should learn all we need to know when we go to market tomorrow, lad," Thad said to Dan's departing back. "You'll be on your way tomorrow night."

"Thank you, sir." And to prove how fit he was, Dan bounded up the stairs two at a time.

Deborah, splashing the dishes in and out of the soapy water, didn't feel as happy as Dan obviously did. Her mind churned over ways of convincing her father that she had a better plan than his. Nat's chirpy whistling as he dried the cutlery nearly drove her distracted. It was so important to get the first sentence right. She looked at her father, sitting with his stockinged feet on the hearth, his chair tilted back, just staring into the flames. It was unusual for him to sit doing nothing. What was he thinking of? Dare she interrupt him? But her mother was out back in the summer kitchen, packing the market baskets. This would be a good time. Better to convince one of them first.

"Father, did you notice how neatly Dan mended the chair?"

"Mmm."

"He seems to be very handy that way. He was hoping to apprentice with his brother for a carpenter before they got tangled up with Mackenzie."

"Mmm."

By this time both Nat and her father were looking at her with cocked eyebrows, but she plunged on regardless.

"He'd be a lot handier about the place than old Tom ever was and there'd be no problem about having to cart him home dead drunk every Saturday night or him just up and taking off without a by-your-leave the way that old bag of bones did."

"Debbie—" her father began, shaking his head.

"Oh, please listen." Her hands, wet from the dishes, sprayed water as she flung them up in front of her to stop his saying no. "It wouldn't be that hard. No one knows he's here. We could easily keep him hidden for two weeks, or a month even, and then dress him up in Nat's good clothes and he could pretend just to arrive at the door one day asking for work."

"My good clothes!"

"Oh, be quiet, Nat. This is important. I don't think he can row across that river without being seen. He'll be shot and what will be the use of our trying to help him at all? Nobody would think for a minute he'd been a rebel if he were dressed properly and we offered him a job and—"

"Debbie, you have a very kind heart, but—"

"Oh, please, Father, please think about it. It would work. I'm sure it would work." And as she said this she hurried the short distance between them to kneel on the floor by his chair. "Please, Father."

The look he gave her was a combination of exasperation and helplessness. "Debbie, we are already suspect. What would the sheriff think if we suddenly acquired a hired man no one had ever set eyes on before?"

"The sheriff. The sheriff!" Deborah beat with her fists on the arm of her father's chair. She swallowed tears that were choking her. "Why couldn't that nosy old man have minded his own business?"

There was silence for a long minute, then her father said quietly, "Alex Hamilton is a good man, Debbie. He is doing his duty as he sees it." He put a finger under her chin and raised her head until she was looking at him with stormy eyes. "And he's doing his duty as *I* see it. I consider what Dan did was wrong. And I consider what we're doing now is wrong. We're helping him because I think he was led astray. But getting him across that river is all we're going to do. Do you understand?"

"Yes, Father," Deborah whispered. But inside, a fiercer Deborah shrieked, "No. No. No!"

10
Stalked

Queenston was in turmoil. Besides the usual market-day bustle, a steamer had arrived from Toronto with two field pieces for the camp springing up at Chippewa, across the river from Mackenzie's self-proclaimed republic on Navy Island.

The Wallbridges were late getting to town that Saturday morning. Usually they all came for the outing, but this time they had argued right through breakfast about what to do. There was no reason why they shouldn't leave Dan alone but ...

Deborah was torn between feeling it was impolite to leave a guest—and in this case possibly dangerous for the guest—and a desperate desire to find out for herself what was going on in the neighbourhood instead of always having to hear things second-hand. However, Father needed Nat to help with the unloading and a woman had to be along to deal with the butter and geese. Finally she had sighed and said, "I'll stay home."

She had felt quite pleased with herself when

she saw her father's smile of approval, so she was amazed to hear her mother say firmly, "No, Deborah, *I* will stay home. Go and collect the baskets. You're late already."

Deborah had turned to look at her mother, ready to protest, and intercepted a meaningful look directed at her father.

"Yes. Well," he said, clearing his throat and pushing back his chair to rise, "your mother's right, Deborah. Come along, Nat. We'll harness up while Deborah collects the market baskets."

It had taken Deborah half the drive to Queenston to puzzle out that her mother thought it improper to leave her alone with Dan.

Once in town they drove straight to the warehouses by the dock to unload their sacks of grain. Deborah stayed sitting on the high wagon seat right beside the steamer, watching the activity around it. The sergeant in charge of unloading seemed to have only four soldiers with him and was busy pressing townsmen into service to roll kegs of gunpowder down the gangplank. Nat went off to help quite willingly after their sacks had been stored away, but Deborah could see Jed Hawkes slouching sullenly against a railing of the steamer until the sergeant barked at him.

As Jed turned to go he caught sight of Deborah. For one heart-stopping moment her eyes were caught by his vicious glare. He bent over the railing and she had to stiffen her back to keep from leaning away. She would not show fear to that bully!

"Just you wait, Miss Stuck-up," he hissed. "We'll get you. I found somethin' real interestin' in that barn of yourn. When the sheriff gets back—"

The sergeant barked again. Jed straightened, his heavy, black brows scowling. "We'll be out to see you," he snarled. "You can count on that." And he lumbered off.

Deborah sat as though frozen to her seat. The hate she had seen in Jed's eyes so shocked her she couldn't begin to think about his words. He *couldn't* still be angry about that silly fight with Nat, could he? But now he had the scene at the Wallbridge house on Monday to hate them for too—he hadn't looked too smart by the time the sheriff had finished with him then. And he *did* hold grudges. She shuddered and pulled her shawl more tightly around her shoulders. What had he meant, something in their barn? Surely Dan would have told them if he had left anything in the barn. Or Nat would have noticed when he was doing the chores. Perhaps Jed was just bluffing.

The clatter of wheels on planking interrupted her. She looked around to see the Crankshaw wagon sweeping into place beside her. Mr. Crankshaw jumped down and flicked the reins over the horse's head to loop them round the hitching rail. Deborah smiled a welcome but Isabella sat rigid, staring straight ahead.

Oh, dear, Deborah thought. What am I going to do? I can't possibly tell her about Dan. Perhaps if I pretend not to notice . . .

114

"Hi, Isabella. Are you going up to Bates'?"

Ordinarily Deborah wouldn't have had to ask. She and Isabella always went to Bates' General Store with their butter, eggs and geese. The Wallbridges, like most people in the township, divided their custom equally between Hawkes' and Bates', but Deborah had always felt uncomfortable under Silas Hawkes' cold stare.

"He's got shifty eyes," she'd once said to her mother.

"Don't be childish, Deborah."

"He's a crook," Deborah had persisted. "I can tell just by looking at him."

"Now that's enough, Debbie," her father had admonished. "You can't go around blackening a man's character just because you don't like the looks of him. It's time you learned to put a bridle on that tongue of yours."

Deborah had said no more, but she held stubbornly to her dislike of the Hawkes. She had talked Isabella into by-passing Hawkes' General Store as well. Trading at Bates' had become the highlight of their week, as she hoped her question would remind Isabella.

Isabella turned only her head toward Deborah. Her black eyes glittered and her mouth was tight. Deborah hoped she could keep her own face smiling and cheerful even though feelings of guilt were tugging down the corners of her mouth. She thought she would never outlast that steely stare, but finally Isabella's glare wavered, became uncertain.

Deborah took a deep breath. "We'll have lots of time to look through their new ribbons and laces. With all that's going on in town today, I'm sure the menfolk will spend ages in the Queenston Arms. I expect we could go now. Your father's just coming out of the warehouse."

Isabella gave her one last, puzzled look, then decided to smile. "All right then," she said. "Let's go."

Deborah was right. They spent several hours by themselves poking about the store, and then were left sitting hunched together on the Crankshaw's wagon, waiting. This was quite common on market days, the women sitting out on the wagons while their menfolk drank in the tavern. Many farmers stopped at every tavern along the road to town, but Deborah's father went only to the Queenston Arms to gather news. Never had she been left sitting until all the other wagons had moved off.

Just as she was considering defying convention and going to look for her father, the door of the hotel opened and Ezekiel Crankshaw appeared with another man, a stranger, or at least not one of their immediate neighbours. Deborah was sure she had never seen him before, yet something about him seemed familiar. He was slightly built but as tall as Ezekiel Crankshaw. A broad-brimmed hat shadowed his features, so all she could make out was a neatly-pointed beard outlining a thin face. Perhaps he had come on the steamer. Then Deborah noticed her father striding along the board sidewalk toward them. He hadn't been in the hotel after all! As he approached, the stranger turned abruptly and disappeared down the alleyway.

Deborah expected her father to comment on such peculiar behaviour, but all he said was, "There you are, Zeke. Well, you were right. There's a lieutenant arrived with orders for the militia to pack the artillery over the Portage Road to Chippewa immediately. I told him it was a sea of mud but he doesn't seem to grasp what that means. He's commandeering wagons and men right now. Nat and I will take our wagon if you would be so good as to take Deborah home."

"He'd best wait a few days to see if the weather turns colder. The carter's wagon bottomed out yesterday and he wasn't hauling anything the like of cannon."

"Yes. Well, you know these regular army types. This lieutenant seems to feel if horses can't do it, men with ropes can. And there *is* some urgency. Somewhere they've learned that Mackenzie has American arms on that island."

"Surely the American government wouldn't be so foolish as to—"

"Who knows where he got them? But MacNab has massed our men within easy firing range of that island and they've nothing but muskets and a few rifles between them and whatever Mackenzie chooses to do."

"Och, MacNab. A seventeen-year-old lieutenant in the last war and he thinks he knows everything there is to know about fighting," Ezekiel Crankshaw snorted.

"He's an up-and-coming man, my friend, and this will push him even higher if he can work it right," Thad remarked drily. "But that's no reason to leave our neighbours to the mercy of his ambition. They need this artillery."

"Quite right. Well, I'll come along with you, but if it looks a hopeless cause I'll not stay." Then they remembered their daughters.

"Don't worry about us," Deborah said quickly. "Isabella and I can drive ourselves home easily enough."

Thad hesitated, then said, "I really think Nat and I must go, Debbie."

Deborah knew what he was trying to tell her—that he and Nat out working with the soldiers and the loyalist segment of the community would be the most effective way to give the lie to any rumours Silas or Jed Hawkes might be trying to start.

"Aye," Ezekiel Crankshaw rumbled, his face impassive. "Best to be seen working for the right side." And apparently not noticing the thunderstruck look on the faces of both Wallbridges, he continued, "You go straight home now, Isabella. No lingering at the Wallbridges. Your mother is too poorly today to be left alone."

"Yes, Pa."

"That goes for you too, Debbie. Hurry straight home. There'll be plenty of light if you don't dawdle. Tell your mother—" He stopped as he saw Isabella's eyes on him, wide and puzzled. "Tell your mother we'll be late but we'll be home tonight for sure. Off with you both now."

Isabella clucked to the horse and started him along Queenston's short main street. As they clattered over the logs set into the road to keep wagons from skidding, Deborah looked back over her shoulder. Both fathers were watching them. Would her father ask for an explanation of that very peculiar remark Isabella's father had made, or would he think it better to leave well enough alone? But that was the second time Ezekiel Crankshaw had sounded as though he knew something he shouldn't. On the other hand, he certainly had no use for Silas Hawkes. Still, the whole thing was unsettling.

They were passing Hawkes' General Store when Deborah straightened around in her seat again. The front door flew open as they drew abreast, and Jed stepped out onto the verandah. He said nothing as they passed, just stood looking after them. Deborah shuddered. Why did he make her flesh crawl? She'd never been afraid of him before.

"That layabout, Jed, got out of work again, I see," Isabella said as she tugged at the reins to turn the horse up the hill. "Bet the big lout snuck off the minute the sergeant turned his back." She glanced sideways at Deborah. "I heard Pa say the Hawkes caused quite a to-do at your place the other day."

"Oh, you know what a liar Jed is. Told the

sheriff he'd seen a rebel crossing our land. Turned out he'd been knocked off Taylor's bridge by someone and made up the story so folks wouldn't think him a fool. Well, he sure looked a fool, I can tell you, sitting in our kitchen contradicting himself all over the place."

"I hope you didn't laugh at him, Deb." Isabella turned a worried face to her friend. "You know what happened that time Tom Hinks laughed at him when he couldn't spell 'melancholy' at the spelling bee."

Deborah remembered only too well how Tom's puppy had ended up in a spring trap set for rabbits. No one had ever been able to prove it was Jed, but he'd gone around looking smug for a week.

"This rebellion business is making enemies out of everyone," Isabella continued sadly. "Drat Mackenzie anyway. And to think he used to live in Queenston. Bad cess to him, I say. If I had the second sight like my Highland granny I'd put a hex on him. Even you and I have been at outs since the whole stupid brangle began."

Reading the double message in this little speech, Deborah felt guilty again. Here she was with her best friend in the whole world and she couldn't trust her with the only interesting secret she'd ever had. But then, it wasn't just a child's game. It could mean Dan's life and her family's livelihood. She sighed. She felt she'd waited forever to belong to the real world, the grown-up world, but she didn't much like this part of it.

"Isabella—" she started. But what could she say that would mend the rift and still not betray her family or Dan?

Isabella looked at her hopefully but Deborah hesitated, remembering the Isabella who chattered on and on and on. A thought no sooner came into her head than it was spoken out loud. With the best will in the world to keep a secret, Isabella would have told someone before nightfall. No, if something had to be sacrificed it would have to be Isabella's feelings. Turning her face from Isabella's pleading eyes, she finished her sentence, "Let me take the reins now." And she reached over and took them from Isabella's rigid hands.

As Deborah was leaning across for the reins, she caught sight of a flutter of movement along the fence that snaked beside the road. "Someone's there," she exclaimed, turning to look behind them.

"Don't be silly. Whoever'd be out here?" Isabella snapped. "Look, you've spooked Patch, jerking at the reins like that. I wish I knew what was wrong with you these days." She hunched her shoulders pettishly away from Deborah.

Deborah sighed and clucked at the horse. Isabella was never in a cross mood for long. Better to let her sulk in silence for a few minutes. She put the sound she had heard out of her mind and set herself to hurrying the horse. There was a woodlot bordering both sides of the road just past Crankshaw's farm lane and she wanted to get through it to her own lane and give Isabella plenty of time to get back again before dark. Dusk came on about four these days and the sky was overcast with a look of snow, making the afternoon grey and gloomy.

She had just flicked the reins again when the horse stumbled to a stop, trembling. "Oh, no. Now what? Here, Isabella, I'll see what it is," Deborah said, handing over the reins as she jumped down. She ran to Patch's head and clucked soothingly until he stopped shifting and snorting. She guessed by the way he was acting he'd picked up a stone and wouldn't move until they'd pried it loose. Even at that, he'd limp for the rest of the day. If they forced him to take her home and then come all the way back to Crankshaw's, he'd be quite lame and Isabella's father would be furious.

Well, first things first, she thought, and nudged her shoulder into the horse's side to keep him from kicking her while she lifted the hoof he was favouring. Just as she'd suspected, a sharp stone was wedged into the quick next to the iron shoe. She couldn't budge it with her fingers.

"What is it?"

"Stone. Throw me the knife." Deborah grunted as the horse shifted sideways.

Isabella leaned over and handed her the stubby knife carried wedged into the side of the wagon for emergencies such as this. Deborah had seen her father and Nat pry out stones any number of times, but she'd never actually done it herself. The awkwardness of holding up the hoof and digging with the knife made her clumsy, and as the stone popped out, the knife slipped and dug into the quick. Patch snorted and shied away from her as a pinprick of blood welled under the point of the knife.

Oh, no, Deborah thought. "Listen, Isabella," she said out loud, "I think you'd better go straight home. You know what your father's like about his horses."

"Deborah, I can't let you go home alone," Isabella protested as they started up again. But when she saw how Patch limped, her insistence on driving Deborah all the way sounded less and less convincing.

"At least come in and we'll hitch up Dapple," she suggested as they reached her farm lane.

"What's half a mile?" Deborah exclaimed, jumping down and pulling the farm baskets after her. "Here, I'll close the gate after you and run the rest of the way. It won't take me ten minutes."

She started off jauntily as the wagon clattered down the lane, but what had seemed a slightly overcast day when she had Isabella with her, suddenly looked sullen and dark. Fifty yards down the road the way ran through the woodlot—a godsend on hot summer days, but now, with the sky darkening, an unfriendly-looking place. Deborah wished there were not quite so much of it. She approached it hesitantly, hating to leave the open fields behind her. The trees towered and arched above her. Even though the branches weren't swaying they seemed to rustle and crack, each sound a pistol shot to her taut nerves.

For goodness sake, be sensible, she scolded herself after she had jumped in alarm for the sixth time. You're frightened, so pick up your skirts and run.

The market baskets on her arm flopped up and down annoyingly, but Deborah felt better running. She could hear nothing but the pounding of her own heart, feel nothing but the wind tugging at her shawl. She turned her face up to the fragments of sky visible through bare branches, breathed deeply, then lurched suddenly as her foot skidded in a wagon rut. She was aware of a twinge in her ankle, her panting breath, and a feeling between her shoulder blades as though someone were behind her.

She whirled. No one. But the road curved slightly. Perhaps they were beyond the bend. If she stood here 'long enough, waited to see who appeared ... Her heart began pounding like a tom-tom.

What on earth are you afraid of? she demanded of herself. You've known everyone in this neighbourhood since you were born. Besides, they'll all be working on the Portage Road by now.

By the time she had caught her breath no one had appeared. "What did you expect?" she said aloud, disgusted with herself. She started walking again as briskly as she could without actually running. The muffled thud of her thick-soled walking shoes and the rustling of branches were all she could hear. The end of the woods was in sight, their gate just beyond. Two minutes. Two minutes and she would be there.

To her overwrought imagination it seemed suddenly darker. She could see candlelight flickering in their window, an eternity down the lane. The very silence as she left the woods was loud in her ears. The gate at last. She had just lifted down the latch rail when a twig snapped loudly. She whirled to face the sound. Nothing. She let out the breath locked in her chest, listening with every nerve. Then a soft, steady crunching as of footsteps started up in the underbrush on the opposite side of the road.

Panic rose in Deborah's throat and choked her. With trembling hands she tore open the gate and ran. The beckoning light seemed never to come closer. Her kilted skirts bunched between her knees and slowed her. She wanted to scream "Mother! Mother!" but the tightness in her chest strangled her. Then suddenly she was on the verandah. The door was open. She was in. She was safe.

11
Showdown

For one horrible moment Deborah thought she was going to cry, burst into noisy, hysterical, choking sobs. She closed her eyes and swallowed. Her mother was holding her tightly, rocking back and forth as they sat side by side on the settle, murmuring the soothing sounds Deborah had not heard since she was a tiny girl. The pounding in her chest quieted.

"I'm all right," she gasped. "I panicked out there. I heard—I heard—" She could go no further. Instead she opened her eyes, to see Dan priming one of their muskets. He stood well back in the chimney nook. The candles that had beckoned her home were trailing smoky wisps from their blackened wicks and the door had been barred. Usually, even at night, they only shot the bolt. Rufus, ears pricked, was pacing back and forth in front of the door, a soft growl grumbling in his throat.

Deborah looked from the door to her mother and Dan. "I thought someone was following me out in the woods."

"Yes, there's someone out there. He threw a rock onto the verandah just as I closed the door. Did you see who it was?" her mother asked.

"No. Just sounds and shadows following me." A violent shudder shook Deborah. Her mother's arms tightened around her again.

"It's all right. It's all right."

"What shall we do?" Deborah whispered, as though whoever was out there might overhear.

"Why are you alone, Deborah? Where's your father? Where's Nat?"

Deborah could hear in her mother's voice the quiver of panic she herself was fighting. Still shaking despite the fire's warmth, she explained about the artillery that had to be hauled over the Portage Road past the Falls to Chippewa.

"But he promised they'd be home tonight no matter what," she finished, hoping to share with her mother that comfort at least. Things never seemed as bad when Father was there.

Her mother sighed and released her hold on Deborah. She stood up and looked uncertainly at the muskets on the table. Was she remembering? Deborah wondered. She had often heard the story of how her mother, a bride of eighteen, had been left alone in the house—little more than a cabin the size of the kitchen—that summer of '13 when the Americans were swarming all over the peninsula. Her husband of three months was with Fitzgibbon at his headquarters in the deCew house—only twenty miles away, but it might as well have been two hundred. She had toiled all spring in the fields only to see the new shoots trampled in the frenzied coming and going that had constituted warfare that strange summer. When they came for her cow she dug in her heels. They would not have it.

A forage party of five men had thundered up to the door, scavenging provisions for the Americans camped at Fort George. She had held them off with two muskets, one fired over their heads and the other pointed straight at the corporal in charge. Deborah always felt that in similar circumstances she would be just as brave. But somehow five ragged, exhausted soldiers twenty-four years in the past didn't seem as terrifying as whatever lurked outside their door tonight. As she watched, her mother's back seemed to stiffen. She was in charge again.

"Load the other muskets, Deborah. Dan, you stay well back out of sight. You're our very last line of defence." As she said this, she was attaching the lead to Rufus's collar.

"Mother, what are you going to do?"

"Rufus and I are going out to see who's there."

"But it might be anybody."

"Perhaps. I think it's Jed Hawkes."

"But he was working with—Oh!" A picture of Jed on the verandah of his father's store, glaring at the two girls as they left town—alone—flashed into her mind. "Yes," she said. "It might very well be Jed." She looked from her mother to Dan.

He stood leaning against the chimney cupboard, the musket cradled across his arms. "Your mother's right," he said quietly. "We can't cower in here all night wondering if something's going to happen." He turned to Mary Wallbridge. "I'll go out the back way and come around the side of the house just in case you need help."

"No. We don't know if he's brought others with him. You might be seen. Now they're just guessing, but if they see you they'll feel justified in doing anything. Deborah, finish loading those muskets and be ready to bring them to me if I call."

Rufus was tugging at the lead. Mary Wallbridge wrapped it around her wrist and lifted down the bar. As soon as she opened the door, Rufus erupted into the grey dusk, barking furiously. Deborah was ready with the muskets as her mother was towed out, pulling back on the lead to control Rufus.

"Quiet!" she commanded, and Rufus was reduced to a low, snarling growl. Deborah hurried over to the door, standing to the side so the glow from the fire wouldn't reveal the muskets.

"Who's there?" her mother's voice rang out from the top step of the verandah. Silence. "Speak up or I'll loose the dog on you."

A figure sidled out of the shadows onto the laneway some distance from the house.

"You pick strange times to come calling, Jed Hawkes. What can I do for you?"

Jed ambled forward until his face was visible in the grey light. Deborah felt her stomach tighten apprehensively, for behind Jed slouched more shadows. If he'd brought a mob with him . . .

"We come for the rebel you got hid."

"You were here with the sheriff, Jed. You know there's no rebel here."

"I know you pulled the wool over the sheriff's eyes," Jed shouted. "We're coming in to look for ourselves."

"You'll get off this land or I'll loose this dog on you."

Deborah felt rather than saw the group edge forward, and ran out the door. Propping one musket within easy reach against the banister, she stood beside her mother on the front steps and raised the other musket to her shoulder. She could see them better out here in the dusk. Only five, but all of them had clubs. Rufus would have been useless by himself if they got a good swing at him. Her mother was talking again, singling out faces from the group.

"Ben Jacobs, what are you doing here? Your father'll have your hide if he ever hears of this. Joe Coutts, is that you back there? Shame on you. You go on home, the lot of you. If I see you around here again, your fathers are going to hear about it."

Two of the figures at the back started to slink away. Another half turned, uncertain.

"What's wrong with you guys?" Jed snarled at his deserting cronies. "You gonna let a woman talk you down? There's a rebel in there, I tell you. We'll be heroes when we drag him back to town. Spread out and we'll rush 'em."

The two retreating figures paused. Deborah tightened her finger on the trigger, looking to her mother for guidance. Mary Wallbridge was reaching down to unhook Rufus's lead. "Stay," she said quietly. Rufus was quivering with anticipation, but he was well trained. He would attack on command or if one of the group rushed them. But what chance did he have against clubs?

Deborah shifted her attention back to Jed's followers. They had paused, half-turned, to listen to him.

"Come on," Jed bellowed. The group hesitated momentarily, then surged forward. They were only ten yards away.

Deborah swung her musket slightly to train it on Jed. "You first, Jed."

Jed froze, then laughed shakily as two of his followers stumbled into him. "Forget her, boys. She's no hand with a gun."

Someone at the back muttered, "You first, Jed." Another snickered.

Deborah glanced quickly at her mother, saw she had the other musket ready in her hands, took a deep breath to steady herself and said, "See that rock at your feet, Jed?" She aimed the musket at a rock not two inches from his boot toe and squeezed the trigger. The musket spat; rock chips flew up. Jed jumped back with a yelp. Two of his companions turned and fled down the lane. The other two were retreating, slowly at first, then faster.

Jed, backing away, raised a fist. "I'll get you for this. I'll bring a posse with guns next time. And torches. We'll smoke that rebel out."

Deborah and her mother stood and watched them stumble and scramble from sight down the lane.

"We'll have to bar that gate," Mary Wallbridge said at last. "Come, Rufus." She started down the steps, the loaded musket still in her hand. Deborah followed, steeling herself not to jump at every shadow, walking briskly, trying to feel as resolute as her mother looked.

The lane seemed endless. They latched the gate and lifted the bar in place, Rufus all the while sniffing around the gatepost and grumbling low in his throat. Deborah looked up, then down, the road. Wherever they had gone they were out of sight, and Rufus wasn't barking, so they couldn't be anywhere too near. Even so, it took almost more courage than she possessed to turn her back on the gate and walk back down the path. By the time they reached the verandah even her mother was running.

As they burst into the house, slamming the door behind them, Dan rose from his crouch at the window. Deborah, collapsing onto the nearest chair, noticed that his hand trembled as he laid the musket down. He gave her a sickly grin.

"Well, we would have accounted for at least two if they'd had a bit more gumption."

"I've never shot at a person before," Deborah said. "I almost couldn't pull the trigger, even though it was Jed Hawkes and I knew I wouldn't hit him."

"You were mighty close." Dan sounded amused.

Deborah sat bolt upright. "I didn't hit Jed because I wasn't aiming at Jed."

Dan said nothing.

"Do you think I can't hit what I'm aiming at?" she demanded, her temper flaring hotly in the aftermath of fright and nerves.

"Well, I—"

"Children!" Mary Wallbridge broke in sharply. "This is no time for quarrelling. We don't know what Jed is doing right now. We have to make plans."

Deborah's spurt of anger died instantly. "What shall we do?"

"I wish I could decide what's best," Dan said at the same time. "I should leave immediately so they have no evidence against you, but with Mr. Wallbridge and Nat away . . ."

"I doubt those louts will be back for a while if at all, and we'll have plenty of warning from Rufus. I agree, Dan, you must leave. But not until it's darker and not until you've eaten. Thank goodness I made stew today. We won't have to start and make something."

All the time she was talking she was ladling it onto plates. Deborah had automatically fetched a loaf from the pantry and begun slicing it. As she worked, her mind sorted possibilities. Reluctantly she abandoned the idea of keeping Dan hidden until the whole silly mess died down. The Hawkes wouldn't give them any peace of mind now. Oh, how she wished they could get even with that dreadful lot! The only other alternative was the boat Nat had found. The ferry was definitely out.

Armed guards patrolled it during the day as it travelled back and forth between Canada and the States, and it was padlocked to the wharf with a sentry mounted all night. That had been one of the bits of news she and her father had picked up in Queenston that morning. Anyone using the ferry was challenged to identify himself if he wasn't known in the neighbourhood.

I wonder if a woman would be challenged? Deborah speculated. She looked at Dan's long, lean frame as he poured boiling water from the kettle into the teapot. He was three or four inches taller than her mother or herself. If they let down the hem of a dress... He hardly had enough of a beard to need to shave every day but would it stand close inspection? He had mostly down on his upper lip. Some women had that. And the last ferry crossing was late in the afternoon, almost dark at this time of year. That meant keeping him hidden for one more day and her mother had said he must leave tonight. But Nat had said that one man alone couldn't let that boat down. It would take two. Two...

"Come, Deborah, this is no time for daydreaming. Dan has to eat and be off."

Deborah sat and bowed her head, only half listening to the rather brief grace her mother used when her husband and son were absent. She found tears springing to her eyes as her mother continued, "And this night especially we pray, watch over thy servant, Daniel, in his time of danger."

Deborah added a particularly fervent "Amen" to that, saying at the same time to herself, but he must have some practical help too.

As they ate, Mary Wallbridge was making plans. "If I draw you a map do you think you can memorize it and find the landmarks in the dark? Some should stand out even at night."

"I'm positive I could. Anyway I'll just have to try. I have a picture in my mind from Nat's description, so I should be all right."

"Nat said there was a patrol close by. You'll have to time them so you'll know when they're farthest from the boat. We'll give you some rags to muffle the oars."

"Father said the sheriff told his men to shoot at anything on the river," Deborah offered reluctantly.

"With luck they won't be able to see me," Dan answered her, "but they might be able to hear me. I'll let it drift for a while before I row."

"There's a bit of a wind," Mary Wallbridge added. "You might find the river choppy."

"I'm sure I can do it, Mrs. Wallbridge. I—" He stopped and looked at both of them intently, as though willing them to understand something he could not put into words. "I can't tell you how I feel about these few days—as though I belonged to a family again. If anything happened to you because of me..."

Deborah realized he was speaking only to her mother now, excluding her. Disappointment rose up and choked her. She swallowed resolutely. I

135

will not cry, she told herself fiercely. I will not cry.

"Thank you for wearing my mother's brooch." Dan was looking at the engraved silver oval pinned at the collar of Mary Wallbridge's dress. "There is no other way I can show you—" He looked down at his plate. "If I—When I get across I might not be able to send you word—a letter might be too dangerous. But somehow, sometime, I'll let you know that it wasn't in vain, what you did for me."

Mary Wallbridge reached over and patted the hand that clutched the edge of the table. "Your mother would have done the same for my son," she said gently. Then briskly, "Now we must make plans. Some warm clothes, to begin with."

12
Flight

Deborah crept down the stairs. A board creaked, making her jump. Silly, she chided herself. She knew no one was in the kitchen—in the house—but she couldn't help peering into every dark corner before taking that last step. Rufus rose from his place by the hearth and came sniffing around her boots. Taking a deep breath, she strode toward the back door, feeling almost buoyant without clinging skirts to trip her up. It wasn't the first time she had worn Nat's trousers. She'd often worn them when riding astride, but she'd had her skirts on over them. Without them was heaven. She must remember to walk like Nat, flinging her legs out from the hip.

Rufus had followed her to the door. Her hand on the latch, she turned to him. "Sit, Rufus. Stay." He cocked his ears enquiringly, his hind quarters quivering but not yet right down. "Stay!" she said, pointing her finger firmly at the floor. He sat, but his eyes seemed to her big with disapproval. "You stay here," she repeated. "I have something to do."

She lifted the latch and tiptoed out through the summer kitchen, past the woodpile to the outside door. Rufus's unhappy whining followed her. Cautiously she opened the door and peered out. Mother and Dan should be in the barn by now. She had debated climbing out a window on the side farthest from the buildings, but she wouldn't have been able to close it and Rufus might have followed. He wasn't terribly willing to obey her.

At least this door was at the back and the barns were to the side. She should be able to circle around to the woodlot and pick up Dan's trail without anyone knowing. Her mother had been afraid Jed might have left a lookout. If he had, she would lead him a merry chase. If not, she could see that Dan got to the boat by the fastest way possible. It was ridiculous to expect him to be able to find his way over strange country in the dark and not run into problems.

She had worked it out quite carefully. There, back and lowering the boat should take only an hour, as she had explained in her note. She hoped her mother could read it. The nib had been soft and she hadn't had time to mend it. Ink had spluttered all over the page. Anyway, her mother would be able to guess where she was. They had argued about it for long enough. Even Dan had refused to let her go, saying sharply (and ungratefully, she thought) that he didn't need her help. She had stopped arguing then, but her mind hadn't been changed. She would help him in spite of himself.

Her mother had decided that, just in case Jed had left someone to spy on them, she and Dan would go out to the barn with milking buckets, Dan's trousers covered by a long apron to give the impression of two women. That meant Deborah must stay out of sight in the house. Once out in the barn it would be easy for Dan to slip into the woodlot and be on his way while Mary Wallbridge did the milking. Before the watcher could realize that only one woman was returning from the barn, Dan would be well away. Deborah thought that part of the plan was very clever, but something else in her insisted that Dan should have a guide.

The idea had come to her when they were all upstairs looking for warm clothes for Dan. She was kneeling among the scattered shirts, folding up the ones too small for either Dan or her brother. They'd fit me, she'd thought suddenly, and then, with rising excitement, "And in boy's clothes I could move fast and be less noticeable." She was so full of her wonderful idea she barely heard her mother going downstairs.

"Tidy up, Deborah, while I see to the milk-pails."

But Deborah was scrabbling in the trunk for trousers, adding more mess to the heaps on the floor, her mind a beehive of plans. It wasn't until Dan came clumping out of Nat's bedroom where he'd been changing that she looked up from her task. Then she had surprised herself by laughing.

Dan was trying to fasten her mother's longest apron around his waist. Deborah could see he'd already had one try at it. The once-starched ties were crumpled and string-like.

"Not like that, silly." Deborah jumped up. "Here, let me do it." She reached for the apron and found instead her hands taken—and held.

"Deborah?" His voice was hoarse.

She could only look at their clasped hands. Sensations entirely new to her were making her heart pound. She could see the tiny pulse in his wrist throbbing.

"If only you didn't have to leave." A lump rose in her throat and she could say no more. She made herself look up. Through her tears his face was a blur, his eyes two diamond points.

"I've never met anyone like you before," he was saying in a tight, uneven voice. "So—so—"

"Intrepid," she supplied with a shaky laugh.

"Wonderful," he corrected almost under his breath. "If only things had been different. If only—"

"Come along, you two," Mary Wallbridge called from below, and they sprang apart instantly.

Deborah was so full of new, unexplored feelings she felt as though she were suffocating. She turned blindly toward the stairs. She would never see him again and she could think of nothing to say, nothing. If only— She paused on the top step and turned back to him just as Dan reached out. He touched, with one finger, the tear sliding down her cheek.

"Don't cry," he said softly. "Don't cry."

She blinked the tears away and looked for one long moment into loving grey eyes. Then her mother called again. But all the way down the dark stairs Dan had held her hand.

She could hardly remember the final flurry of leave-taking, but as Dan and her mother had gone out the kitchen door she had shaken herself out of her bemused trance and sped upstairs to change. Now, more than ever, she was determined to see him safely across the river.

If Father had been here it would be different, Deborah told herself as she slipped away from the house. But as it is, there's only me to show him the way if he's going to get there quickly. Crouching in the shadow of a tree, her eyes growing more accustomed to the dark each minute, she wondered if Dan had left yet. She could hear her mother in the barn, see the glow from the lantern. Methodically she scanned the buildings. Her mother would have shown him the connecting door from the barn to the driveshed. From there he could easily slip out into the shadow of the old cabin, used now as a smokehouse and piggery.

Deborah's eyes followed the trail she imagined for Dan and came to rest on the last in the string of outbuildings just as a shadow thickened and took shape in the elbow of the wall. Short and humped, it loped into the open momentarily, then faded into the shadowy bushes that lined the snake fence.

Deborah smiled to herself and settled back on

her heels. That's what she'd do too. Bend double and run in the shadow of the fence. But not yet. She had no intention of catching up with Dan until it was too late for him to send her back.

Squatting on her heels, she forced herself to count to one hundred. That should give him enough of a start.... Eighty-nine...ninety...He wouldn't need her help until he was on Crankshaw land. That's where the landmarks were deceiving...Ninety-nine...one hundred. Now.

She took a deep breath and crept forward, dodging from tree to tree until she reached the edge of the woodlot. Thank goodness there was still some muffling snow. She reached the snake fence without so much as a twig snapping. Clever of her mother to suggest walking inside the fence where Dan's footprints would be lost in a welter of others on this much-used path. The fence was only waist-high, but the bushes that grew in the zigs and zags made it a ragged foot or two taller. Running crouched, she should look like a bush stirring in the breeze, if anyone was watching.

Running bent over was hard on the back. She felt disoriented and uneasy looking at the path instead of keeping watch around her. She stopped beside a particularly large bush to ease her back. Dan should be near the end of their property by now. If it were daylight she'd be able to see him, a speck in the distance where the fences crossed. Tonight, with cloud cover dimming the light of moon and stars, she could see nothing beyond the pale line of fence directly before her.

She started forward again, not quite so quietly now because the crisp air was making her breathe raggedly. But she couldn't slow down. Once Dan started across Crankshaw land she could only guess his precise direction unless she was close enough to spot him. She put forth an extra spurt of speed. Dan couldn't be much farther ahead. She could vaguely see the surveyor's corner stake jutting up beyond the next clump of bushes.

As she hurried toward it, something caught her foot and sent her sprawling full-length. She landed heavily, the wind knocked out of her. Gulping air, she was pushing herself up on her elbows when she was lifted by the back of the jacket. Instinctively she kicked backwards. Her assailant swore and dropped her so that she staggered forward before being grabbed and twirled around.

"Dan! Dan, it's me," she gasped, flinging up both hands between her face and his clenched fist.

In the dim light she could see only the whites of his eyes, staring. Suddenly she was grabbed again and shaken ferociously.

"How dare you, Deborah?" he hissed at her through clenched teeth. "How dare you just ignore what we told you? How many times do you have to be told? This is no game. I'm not running around out here for the fun of it."

"Stop, Dan. Please, stop," Deborah just managed to say. She grabbed at his wrists. Fury subsiding, his arms dropped to his sides and his shoulders sagged.

"Now what am I going to do?" he asked bleakly.

"I came to help you."

"I don't need any help," Dan said, biting off every word.

A feeling of rejection slashed through Deborah, leaving her trembling. Justifications welled up in her—she could show him the exact place, he would need someone to help lower the boat—but she could not force them past her stricken throat.

"Come on," he said at last. "I'll take you back."

"Wait, Dan. Please let me explain. In ten minutes we could be at the boat if you'd let me show you the fastest way."

Without saying a word he turned her around and propelled her in front of him back down the path they had just covered. Several yards along, she dug in her heels and they bumped to a stop.

"There is no danger to me out here, Dan. Even if someone sees us there's no danger."

"Not even Jed?"

"What would he be doing skulking around the back half of Crankshaw land at this hour of the night?"

"If there's no danger out here, why do I need your help?" Dan demanded harshly.

Deborah swallowed the hurt that welled up in her throat again. "To lower the boat. Nat said it would take two."

Dan passed one hand over his face, squeezing tightly at his temples as though to relieve pain.

"Come on then," he said finally, and stalked back down the path toward the surveyor's stake.

A few minutes later their shadows rippled across the frozen furrows of Crankshaw's back acres and faded into the trees that fringed the river road. They paused for several seconds to listen up and down the road, then glided across and snaked into the scrub on the other side. Here it was more difficult to be quiet. The verge had never been cleared. Deborah felt their progress through the twig-strewn underbrush must sound like an army firing volleys as it moved.

Dan's hand on her arm stopped her. "How much farther?" he whispered right in her ear.

"Maybe fifty yards," Deborah decided, trying to visualize the countryside as it would be in daylight. "And then straight down twenty feet, gradually at first and then very steeply. It's gullied, so we'll slip if we don't use the trees as handholds."

Dan still hesitated. "Deborah, I wish you'd go back now. You've shown me the place. I can't bear to take you into further danger. Please go back."

"Nat said it would take two to lower the boat," she reminded him, wondering to herself at the same time, why do I keep insisting that I must go right to the river? Am I just, as Nat keeps telling me, plain pig-headed? But I want so desperately to see him safely across. "Even with me it's going to be noisy. Without me you'll have to drop it in. It'll sound like a cannon going off when it hits the water. And if it drifts before you can get down—"

"There must be some way of tying it."

"How will you untie it once you're in the boat?"

"With my knife," he said impatiently, then paused. "I forgot, I lost it. But there's a knot I can do. That isn't a problem. Will you please go back?"

Deborah didn't answer.

"Why must you be so stubborn?" he whispered fiercely.

"The longer we argue the less chance you have of getting away."

He let his breath out in a long, exasperated hiss, then said, "I'm not as ungrateful as I sound. I'll be . . . anxious . . . for you alone back here once I'm on the river. Promise you won't wait, you'll head straight back as quickly as possible?"

The concern in Dan's voice brought tears to Deborah's eyes. Why does he have to leave? Why? one part of her mind demanded, while the rest fought down the emotion engulfing her.

Finally her voice was steady enough to say, "Yes, I promise—if you promise to write from wherever you end up and let me know what happened."

"Yes. I'd like very much to write to you. I—"

She thought he was going to say more. She searched his face, a pale oval against the black tree shadows, and could read nothing on it. Every line and pucker was obscured by the fluid darkness. Finally his hand tightened on her arm but all he said was, "Let's go."

They moved along the top of the embankment first, where the trees were sparser, but at last, reluctantly, had to plunge down into the thicker growth. Years of playing hide-and-go-seek with Nat and Isabella had taught Deborah to lean her weight on the sloping tree trunks, testing the ground lightly with one foot before transferring her weight forward. Dan too seemed to be good at the noiseless zig-zagging from tree to tree. They made only a slight rustling on their way down the gentle slope. Deborah held up her hand when they reached the steeper bit and Dan came to crouch beside her.

"Watch out for tree roots," Deborah said into his ear, and was about to explain about the deeply-eroded gullies below them when a scraping sound made them freeze. Scarcely daring to breathe, Deborah strained to hear. Rustling. An animal in a bush, she thought. She leaned over to whisper to Dan but he put a finger to her lips. The scraping sound came again, from farther away.

Beyond them was the black glisten of the river and soft lapping sounds, but the ground cut away too abruptly below for them to see the shore, even if there had been more light. Dan shifted sideways toward a tree that slanted out over the river. Taking his weight on his hands, he inched along it until he could lean out over the embankment. Just as he had lowered himself full-length on the trunk there was a scrabbling of pebbles and a voice rang out.

"Who's there? Stand and be recognized or I'll shoot."

Deborah felt a sickening lurch in her stomach. Dan seemed frozen to the tree. For an eternal second there was dead silence, then another voice boomed.

"Hold your fire, John. It's Ezekiel Crankshaw."

Deborah was beyond rational thought. She could only crouch where she was, listening to sounds erupting around her—boots crunching over gravel, scrambling over rock, then voices again and, with them, vague shadows far below.

"What're you doing out here at this time of night, Zeke? I might've shot your head off."

"You might've tried. And I'll ask you the same thing, seeing as you're on my land."

"Patrollin' the river bank. Thought I heard somethin' so I came a bit further'n usual. And you?"

"Don't see as I have to answer for what I do on my own land. Fact is, doing your business for you. Coming home from that damn fool nonsense up on the Portage Road, thought I saw a light. Must've been imagining things. Haven't seen a blessed soul. Come on. I'll walk back a piece with'ee. Easier to scramble up back your way."

Deborah couldn't hear the answer as the two men moved off. Her heart, which had seemed to stand still while they talked, was now beating violently in her ears. She had to stand up or fall over. Painfully she straightened, easing herself up against a tree trunk. Dan was inching backwards from his perch. Hand over hand he brought himself back to a knee-crouch, then reached backwards with one foot for support on the ground.

Deborah had straightened herself off her supporting tree and was gathering her breath to whisper to him when she was grabbed from behind. Strong fingers sealed her mouth, an arm pinioned her against a heavily-coated body. For a second she went slack from fright, then gathered herself together and stamped hard where a foot should be. She felt the figure jerk as the heel of her boot dug in. The slight grunt alerted Dan. He spun around.

Run! Run! Deborah was screaming inside her head. She jerked sideways, trying to signal Dan to get away, but he stood, his hands raised in fists, and just stared, as though mesmerized, at Deborah and her captor.

13
Explanations

Deborah could hear the rasp of flint on file. A glint of sparks dazzled her eyes momentarily, then the soft glow of a lantern lit the three faces in front of her and cast long shadows into the mow of Ezekiel Crankshaw's barn.

"Well, that was a stroke of luck. Here we are trying to figure out how to get our hands on you and you walk right into them." Deborah's assailant grinned at Dan, his pointed beard fox-red in the subdued light. The man at the hotel, Deborah realized. "Thought we were going to have to walk right up to Thad Wallbridge's door."

"But how did you know?" Dan was still wearing that dazed look that had so frustrated Deborah on the embankment, but he certainly had no fear of this man.

"Zeke here spotted Mother's brooch, remembered mine, and put two and two together. Otherwise we'd still be running around like chickens with no heads."

So that's who he was. No wonder she'd thought she knew him.

"But why were you down at the boat?"

"To see if it was still there. If it was gone I'd have tried tracking you on the American side." He grasped Dan by both shoulders, smiling. "It's a relief to see you, I can tell you."

"But how do you get back and forth so easily?" Deborah blurted out. "Are you a spy or something?"

Matthew turned and looked at her speculatively. "Ah, yes. Little Miss Wallbridge. Now how do you come to be poking into this business?"

Deborah could feel her cheeks flushing and her temper rising at the acidic tone of his voice, but before she could fling back a retort Dan rushed to her defence.

"It was Deborah who found me in the barn and talked her family into helping me. I'd be dead of the cold by now if it weren't for her."

"Then we must say thank you and return her home as quickly as possible." The voice still had an edge to it.

Deborah was so angry she could feel her teeth grinding. How could he look so like Dan and be so unlike? Ezekiel Crankshaw's voice cut across her thoughts.

"Aye, we'd best be off before anyone thinks to check why there's a light in this barn at close on nine of the evening. I'll take the lass home. Can you sneak your brother into your hotel room?" As Matthew nodded, Ezekiel added, "And give him a haircut. That'll make him look respectable enough to pass as your apprentice on the ferry tomorrow."

"The ferry!" Deborah exclaimed. "They're questioning everyone on the ferry."

"Everyone they don't know. I travel it constantly."

"But you're a rebel too. Why shouldn't they suspect you of spying for Mackenzie or...or—" She couldn't think what else he might be doing.

She saw his face muscles tighten, giving him a hard, cold look. "You already know more than is good for any of us."

"Matthew," Dan interrupted suddenly, "I think she has a right to know."

"One word from her," Matthew reminded him grimly, "and Zeke here goes to jail—or worse."

Deborah stood mute, stunned that anyone would think her so base, but Dan erupted hotly. "If she were like that, I wouldn't be here."

"I didn't mean she'd tell on purpose. It only takes a careless word or two these days." Matthew passed a hand wearily over his face. "Look, we have to get out of here. Zeke?"

"You tell the lass whatever you want to tell her, lad," Ezekiel said gruffly. "And then we can all be off."

Dan turned to Deborah and almost absent-mindedly took hold of her hands as he talked. "I explained to you how we feel, Matthew and I, about the government abuses. Well, Matthew can move about the country easily doing his work so he's been able to find out how other people feel as well. And he does a lot of carpentry for people in Lewiston and Buffalo too, so he's been able to find out how American sympathies lie. It was very important for Mackenzie to know how much backing he had, so Matthew's crossed a lot lately. The people at the ferry dock won't think twice about him crossing again tomorrow."

"But if he was seen at Toronto with the rebels that day?"

"I doubt anyone saw him. He'd been away on a trip when the call came. He only got back in time to come and find me when the fracas had already started."

"And to give you a flea in your ear for being such a cawker," Matthew said with an exasperated grin for his brother. "Anybody with half an eye could see the thing wasn't going to work. The organization was falling apart at the top."

"You mean you weren't going to risk your own skin!" Deborah rounded on him, all the turmoil of the last few hours loosening her tongue disastrously. "You weren't willing to stand up and be counted for a cause you believed in, the way Dan was."

Deborah found she was shaking uncontrollably as Matthew straightened grimly out of his slouch, but all he said was, "There are more ways to fight a war than deliberately walking into the path of a bullet. It's time we were away."

Deborah turned to look at Dan just as Ezekiel doused the candle. What could she say to him? As she tried to sort out her thoughts she heard a rustling as of paper and Matthew said, "Zeke, take this. If the Wallbridges have any trouble, use it. I certainly owe them that much." And while she was still puzzling that out, Matthew swept Dan out of the barn in one direction while Ezekiel Crankshaw urged her in the other.

"We'll have to walk across the fields, lass," was the first and last thing he said until they were walking up her farm lane and she could see her father on the verandah, arms folded grimly, waiting.

Noon dinner was over the next day before Ezekiel Crankshaw returned with the news. When his horse clattered into the yard, Deborah was quietly clearing the table, being careful to give her father no particular reason to notice her. There had been five anxious seconds last night out on the verandah when she had been afraid he was going to forget that she was too old to be spanked. Despite the hugs that had followed, she knew it wouldn't take much, now that the fright and relief at having her back safely were over, to remind her parents they were mighty annoyed with her. So, even though her stomach was tightening nervously, she did not run out and demand to know that Dan was safe.

Instead she watched her father going out the door, and thought about Ezekiel Crankshaw's strange revelations of the night before. Once the story of Dan's rescue had been explained to her parents, there had been an awkward silence while they all sat and wondered about the connection between a proclaimed rebel and a neighbour who, as far as they knew, was a loyal citizen. Ezekiel Crankshaw himself had broken the silence.

"Well, now," he had said, rasping one hand down his long, bony face. "You'll be wanting to know about my tie-up with Matthew Peterson."

"That's your own business, Zeke," Thad Wallbridge had said, while Nat, behind his father's back, had rolled his eyes at Deborah in comic protest.

"Aye, it is. But I'll mebbe be telling you anyway. You mind my lad Angus?" he said abruptly. And when they all nodded, "Well, some months ago—May, if I mind it right—Matthew Peterson fetched up on my doorstep with word Angus was out west in the Red River settlement. He had a letter for me. It said—well, no matter what it said. But my lad'll be home by spring." He finished up quickly and looked ready to bolt when Mary Wallbridge put her hand on his arm.

"Mr. Crankshaw, I'm so happy for you."

Thad just buffeted him on the arm in that wordless way of expressing emotion that Deborah had noticed before in men. Ezekiel Crankshaw's craggy features lightened momentarily.

"The lad seems to have done well out west," he offered at last. "Grown up, I dare say. But that's neither here nor there. The point is, that's how I came to know Matthew Peterson." He looked Thad right in the eyes. "I knew he was smuggling the odd chest of tea and tobacco and I suspected he was spying for Mackenzie, but I was willing to turn a blind eye."

Deborah saw her father's eyebrows rise in that quizzical way he had, but he said nothing, just pulled thoughtfully at his pipe and, surprisingly, Ezekiel continued.

"Those Family Compact fellows up in Toronto —calling themselves Members of the Legislature! Too full of themselves by half, they are," he stated. "I mind what happened in the old country when the government got too high and mighty. Thought they could treat people like cattle. My family thrown off a holding we'd farmed a hundred years so the laird could have the land for sheep. We were barely out the door when his men set fire to the house. All we could see up and down the glen was smoke from houses on fire. My mother and sister starved to death before my father and I found work. And we were the lucky ones. Whole families died at the side of the road, tramping from one village to another looking for work. It could happen here." He was sitting hunched over, his bony hands clasped between his knees, staring into the fire.

Deborah felt as though she and everyone in the room were holding their breath, waiting. She had lived on the next farm to this man all her life and yet had known none of these things about him. As she stared at him, wondering, he shook himself out of his trance and continued scornfully.

"As for this lot we've got governing us—petty merchants, government time-servers. Not even landed gentry. It's time someone gave them a sharp prod. I don't hold with armed revolt, mind, but those farmers out back of Toronto have just complaints. Any road, I wasn't about to put a spoke in Matthew Peterson's wheel. And when he fetched up here a week ago looking like something the cat dragged in, I said I'd keep an eye out for his brother."

"Has he been hiding in your barn all this time, Mr. Crankshaw?" Nat piped up from his seat on the hearth.

Deborah thought for a moment Ezekiel wasn't going to answer. He stroked his chin and snapped his ferocious brows together, then seemed to come to some decision.

"Naw, naw. There's a man wouldn't stay holed up anywhere for long. He was off to Chippewa where he rents a room, and changed his clothes. Walking the streets of Queenston bold as brass the next morning, he was. But he couldn't be asking around openly after his brother. Then he heard the stories that son of the devil, Silas Hawkes, was spreading about. Well, he was in a rare pickle. Come hightailing it out to my place with the tale. I said straight off, 'You're daft, man. If there's a rebel on Thad Wallbridge's land, he doesn't know about it.'"

He shot his neighbour a challenging look and to Deborah's amazement her father's face reddened under its weatherbeaten tan. "Reckon we've all been caught out in a thing or two, at some time or other," he muttered around the stem of his pipe.

"Any road," Ezekiel continued, "thought it wouldn't hurt to pay a visit and pass on the local

157

gossip—and a warning, just in case." He sat nodding his head for so long that Nat finally prodded him.

"Well, what did you find out, Mr. Crankshaw?"

"Nothing very helpful. Young Deborah there seemed a mite agitated, but it had been an unsettling sort of week. I thought there was something familiar about that brooch." He indicated with a lift of his chin the brooch still at Mary Wallbridge's throat.

"I saw you looking at it," Deborah said. "It gave me a nasty turn."

"Daresay I gave you more than one nasty turn the last while," Ezekiel said with what sounded to Deborah remarkably like a snort of laughter.

"Indeed you did, Mr. Crankshaw," Deborah's mother assured him. "The brooch must have told you Dan was here. Why didn't you just say right out?"

"I wasn't sure about the brooch till I'd met up with Matthew again on market day. I was all for asking you then, Thad, but Matthew favoured a more roundabout way. Not a trustful man, Matthew Peterson. But in these times who can blame him. I knew if you'd taken the boy in you wouldn't turn around and hand him over to the sheriff. But Matthew had seen old Silas rampaging about and he was scared for young Dan. That reminds me. If you have any trouble with that greasy hellhound—" Ezekiel growled, turning directly to Thad. Then he seemed to think again. "Well, no matter. We'll not worry about that yet. Daresay you're glad it's all over."

"I am that," Thad acknowledged. "But there's still tomorrow morning to worry about."

Deborah's father and Ezekiel had decided between them that it would be best if the Wallbridges stayed quietly at home the next day. Farm families didn't often miss church on winter Sundays when the roads were hard enough for easy driving and the farm work had slackened off, but since Thad and Nat had been out until all hours slugging heavy artillery over the Portage Road, no one would wonder at their absence.

Ezekiel, however, had every intention of driving *his* family to church. The ferry to Lewiston would be leaving just as they were driving past. Deborah imagined the scene to herself through a long, wakeful night: Dan and Matthew boarding, the ten-minute crossing, then disembarking in the States, free—safe! She had fallen asleep with that scene in her mind, only to wake suddenly in the middle of a nightmare: Dan being dragged from the boat by a ghastly Silas, his eyes glowing like hot coals. With talon-like hands he was tearing at a frantically writhing Dan . . .

For the rest of the night she lay shivering and wide awake. When dawn finally came she crept from her bed and plunged into the morning tasks. She had breakfast steaming on the table by the time the rest of the family appeared. And now, an endless morning and another meal later, hollow-eyed and exhausted, she was scrubbing at the dishes, desperate to know what had happened.

Would the men never come in from that barn? She rammed a dish into its drying slot. There, that was the last of them. She dried her hands and picked up the basin. Throwing the water outside in the winter was a good way to get the croup, but she didn't care. She was going to do it anyway. Basin on hip, she opened the door to see the men sauntering up from the barn. Her pulse leaped in anticipation as she tipped the water over the side of the verandah. Just then Ezekiel Crankshaw caught sight of her.

"Be easy, lassie," he bellowed, and then as they came within speaking distance, "Your wee man is safe across."

Deborah could feel her knees start to shake. She knew she must sit down or fall down. Without a word she turned and stumbled inside. She was still sitting on the bench by the door, the basin clutched on her lap, when they came stamping in. Her mother came downstairs and Deborah, sitting dazed by the doorway, pieced together the story from the jumble of questions and answers as the men sat down to a mug of ale.

It was almost disappointingly tame. The Crankshaws had driven along the river road approaching Queenston just as the ferry pulled out. Ezekiel could see red-bearded Matthew standing at the railing a little way off from the rest of the passengers. At his side stood a neat and freshly-barbered figure.

As Ezekiel watched, the ferry had reached the halfway mark, the boundary between Canada and the United States. The two figures standing at the back of the ferry had each raised an arm in farewell, whether to him or to their homeland he didn't know. They had both turned, after that single gesture, and walked to the front of the ferry as though ready to face the future.

Deborah's eyes were brimming with tears as Ezekiel's deep voice rolled out that last word. She picked up the basin and walked carefully back into the summer kitchen before letting the tears spill over. If only she could have said something more to him last night—what, she didn't know. If only it hadn't ended with her turning on his brother—the answer, after all, the perfect answer to their problem. If only he would write. She had no way of tracing him. If he didn't make the first move—

Why was she crying? He was safe. They were all safe. But she could not stem the sobs that rose and choked her. Muffling the sounds with her apron, she crumpled onto the floor of the cold, back room, put her head down on the wooden bench and gave way to a misery she only half understood. She was spent with crying and half asleep in her uncomfortable crouch when the sounds of someone arriving roused her.

14
Standoff

Deborah's first thoughts were for her red eyes. It might be Isabella or someone else who would ask for her, and if Nat noticed her puffy eyes he would tease. She dipped the corner of her apron into the barrel of water kept for washing dishes, and patted her eyes. The cool wetness soothed her headache as well. That would have to do. Taking a deep breath to calm herself, she marched into the kitchen.

At first she couldn't see who had come. Her father's broad back blocked her view. She could see only Ezekiel Crankshaw where he sat glowering at someone, his eyebrows forming one broad, black slash across his furrowed forehead.

"Well, spit it out, man. Let's hear what you have to say," her father barked.

Deborah sidled around to have a better look, and her heart jolted against her ribs painfully. At the far side of the table sat Jed and Silas Hawkes. Why am I frightened? she asked herself. There's nothing they can do, now. But her chest constricted anyway when Jed threw her a malevolently triumphant look.

Silently she crept farther into the room, past the rocker where her mother sat knitting, and perched herself next to Nat on the hearthstone. He made a "What now!" face at her, but she was too tense even to shrug her shoulders. She jumped convulsively as her father's hand smacked down on the table.

"I'm fed up with this harassment. Say what you've come to say and get out."

"I'll say it, all right," Silas gloated. "We've got you dead to rights, Wallbridge. Real evidence. Jed found it in your barn. I got dogs out there. We're hunting your rebel out right now."

"You're what?" Thad roared. He jumped to his feet and in one quick movement had snatched a musket and trained the barrel on Silas. "Get out of my house," he ordered between clenched teeth.

Silas started to sputter a protest but Ezekiel interrupted.

"Hold on, Thad. Sit ye down, man. We'll be having to talk this through."

To Deborah's amazement her father, after a long, hard look at his neighbour, sat down, but he was still breathing rapidly and the musket rested across his knees. It would take very little to make him explode.

As the tension subsided, Ezekiel tipped his chair back and hooked his thumbs through his suspenders as though settling in for a friendly chat. "You're mighty free with those dogs after the to-do in town this morning," he began conversationally.

He paused until all eyes were on him, Silas's bulging with suppressed fury. "Oh, yes, I was about when the sheriff was telling ye he'd no more time for your half-baked notions. Now, if he wouldn't be listening t'ye, why should we?"

"He'll listen," Silas hissed. "He'll listen. I've proof. And when those dogs're finished I'll have proof positive."

"And just what might this proof be?"

Ezekiel Crankshaw seemed to have taken over. The rest of them, Deborah noticed, were just looking, open-mouthed, from one speaker to the other. Now all eyes were on Silas. He snapped his bony fingers under his son's nose and Jed suddenly came to life, dug into his breeches pocket and dropped a clasp knife onto the palm of his father's outstretched hand.

Without moving a muscle Silas said, "There's your proof. That come outa your barn the day after the sheriff was here. Outa the haymow. Saw somethin' else too." Silas leaned forward, his eyes darting, weasel-like, from face to face.

He's just loving every minute of this, Deborah thought while she stared mesmerized at the bristles that stuck straight out from Silas's protruding chin. She had actually started to count them when Silas rasped again.

"What else? Blood! Blood from a wound and a spot all packed down where someone was lying," he ended triumphantly, and plunked the knife down on the table in front of Thad Wallbridge.

164

Thad took a deep breath. "Blood in a barn? Not unusual. Neither is a clasp knife. Nat here has at least two he probably can't put his hand on this minute."

For answer Silas reached out and flipped the knife over. Cut into the wooden body were the initials *D.P.* Deborah gasped but quickly turned it into a cough.

"Don't reckon to find your boy walkin' around with *D.P.* decoratin' his knife," Silas sneered.

"Don't reckon to find your boy walking round with it either."

"You know why he had it."

"I can guess. He picked it up somewhere."

"He picked it up in your barn."

"Did you see him?"

"What?"

"Did you see him? Did anyone see him?" Thad waited while Silas thought that through, then said, "All you know is your boy came home with someone else's knife."

"You calling my boy a liar?"

"Look, Silas, there's no proof that knife was ever in my barn or on my property. And if it was, what then? Who is this D.P. anyway?"

"Who cares who he is," Silas snarled. "He's a rebel and he's here. Those dogs'll flush him out."

Just then Rufus rose growling as the yelping of several dogs came closer.

"There, you see!" Silas jumped up, his face splitting in a thin-lipped grin. The chair he'd been sitting on crashed over backwards but the sound was lost under Rufus's hysterical barking. Nat just managed to grab the dog's collar before Silas flung the door open. Cold air whistled in. The fire started to smoke but it was ignored in the general rush for the door. Deborah and her mother ended up at the window as the men crowded out the doorway.

Coming up from the barn were three men Deborah knew slightly. The lead man, Tom Jameson, raised hunting dogs. Each man grasped two leashes, at the ends of which strained liver-coloured hounds. They yipped softly, fanning out every so often to follow trails that seemed interesting.

Silas Hawkes bounded down the verandah steps toward them, shrieking, "Well! Well! What'd you find?"

Deborah could see her father and Ezekiel Crankshaw standing shoulder to shoulder on the top step, ready to take on the whole boiling bunch, she thought with a surge of pride. Nat, one hand muzzling Rufus, was jammed into the doorway with Jed. They couldn't decide whether to glare at each other or watch the drama unfolding.

"Speak up. Speak up. What'd you find?" Silas's voice rose higher with each word.

"Nothing," the lead man growled. "Not a damned thing."

"What? What? Y'must have. Get back there and look again!"

"Who're you ordering about, Hawkes? If we didn't find nothin', there's nothin' to find. Sorry about this, Mr. Wallbridge, but Silas there, he come out with sheriff's orders."

"Sheriff's orders?" Ezekiel Crankshaw rumbled. "Reckon you've been duped, man. Sheriff wasn't giving yon blatherskite orders to call out dogs when I heard him this morning."

"That right, Silas? You bin making a fool o' me?"

"Sheriff was busy this morning or he'd of been out here himself," Silas blustered, but Ezekiel interrupted drily.

"He was all but telling ye t'gae t'the devil, man!"

Silas rounded on Ezekiel furiously, but before he could say anything Tom Jameson shouted, "Trying t'make me look bad, were you, Hawkes? Don't you come asking for these dogs again without you've written orders or I'll set 'em on *you*. Come on, boys. Let's get out o' here."

As they strode toward their horses, Thad leaned down and grabbed Silas Hawkes by the collar of his coat. "Silas," he said through clenched teeth, "I am going to throw you off my property with my own two hands." He twisted the material tighter as Silas began to squirm, but before he could do anything Ezekiel spoke.

"Nay, Thad, nay. Let's be hauling him inside here. We've more t'settle with yon blatherskite."

Jed and Nat backed quickly into the house as the men, dragging Silas, strode toward the door. Deborah and her mother stood amazed, not moving from the window, while Silas was dumped

167

into a chair, whining, "What is this? What is this?" over and over.

"Now then, neighbour Hawkes," Ezekiel rumbled, setting himself firmly on his chair. He leaned forward with the most terrifyingly stern look Deborah had ever seen on that ferocious face. "We've some business to be talking with you. Nasty things have been happening around here the while. You've been over-quick to point an accusing finger round this neighbourhood. 'Tis time you stopped."

"Bluff. All bluff," Silas squawked. "You can't frighten me." He pulled himself up straighter in his chair, a touch of his old swagger returning. "I'll have you up in court for intimidation, defamation of character, the whole lot of you. You'll be ruint."

"And what about you, Silas, when your midnight activities be known?"

"You're full of hot air, Crankshaw." Silas made to rise but was clamped back down by a huge hand.

"Just you be looking at something here, my wee mannie." Ezekiel dug into his breeches pocket and produced a square of paper folded in four. From the pink and blue lines crisscrossing it, Deborah could tell it had been torn from a ledger, the kind shopkeepers record their transactions in.

"'Twas careless of you, Silas, to be signing a receipt for the last consignment. Cash on the barrelhead was good enough for your regular man."

Silas had turned ashen and crumpled on his chair when Ezekiel produced the paper. Deborah, in total bewilderment, looked from Ezekiel to Silas to her father, on whose face a smile was growing for the first time in days.

"Tobacco and tea," Ezekiel announced, holding up the note. "Delivered once a month at the dark of the moon."

"Where did you get that?" Silas croaked.

"What? No denials? Would ye be admitting now—" Ezekiel was beginning, when Jed suddenly lunged forward and tore the note from his fingers. In a single motion he turned and flung it on the fire. The paper crackled briefly, curled, and crumbled into brown flakes.

"So much for that," Jed smirked.

"That's my boy. That's my boy!" Silas was his cocky self again. He bounded over to put an arm around his son. "Well, Crankshaw. What d'you say now, eh? Where's your evidence?"

"The five of us saw it, Silas," Thad reminded him. "And you all but admitted the truth of it."

"Your word against mine," Silas scoffed. "What good is that?"

"Five witnesses against one of you."

"A plot—collusion! That's what any court would call it. You can't scare me. You've no concrete evidence."

"For that matter, you've no concrete evidence for your charges either. There's no way you can ever prove anyone was on my land that didn't have a perfect right to be here."

Silas's eyes lost some of their triumphant gleam.

"And what's more," Thad continued, "there's

169

plenty of folks who'd be willing to believe what I could tell them about you. It might not stand up in court, but once people start watching you, you'll find it mighty hard to get away with your little tricks." He let that sink in for a minute before adding, "Shall we call it a standoff?"

With a violent oath Silas grabbed his hat from the table and stomped to the door. Jed, looking neither right nor left, rushed after him. Not until the door crashed shut behind them did anyone in the kitchen move.

Deborah could contain her feelings no longer. "It's not fair," she burst out. "It's not fair! He got away with it! He's bullied people around here for years. Now we have proof he buys smuggled goods and he gets away with it."

Her father looked at her with tired eyes. "No, it's not fair. He's a cheat and a liar and this neighbourhood would be better off without him. But how can we point an accusing finger at Silas Hawkes after what we've been doing? Many things Silas has done are wrong, but in trying to ferret out a rebel he had the law on his side."

The fire died out of Deborah's eyes. She felt tired, defeated and grown-up. According to everything she had been taught in church, what they had done was right and what the Hawkes had done was wrong. Why couldn't right just be right and wrong be wrong? Her shoulders sagged.

Her father came over and put his arms around her. "I know, Debbie. I know," he said as though reading her mind. "It's an odd world where an act of mercy is wrong and an act of malice is right. I told you once that what we were doing was wrong. Well, I've changed my mind—no matter *what* the law says."

Deborah felt a burden melt away. Her heart lifted. She *had* done the right thing. Surely everything would work out.

15
1843: The wanderer returns

Dan was on the ferry half an hour before departure time. He dropped his satchel on the deck by the forerailing and put the wooden tool box carefully beside it. That was his passport to a new life, that tool box—everything he needed to set up as a master carpenter. And the other passport...
He patted his coat front just to hear the crackle of paper in the pocket. He didn't need to take it out to look at it. He knew every word, every flourish of the pen, by heart.

VICTORIA, by the Grace of God, of the
United Kingdom of Great Britain and Ireland,
Queen, Defender of the Faith, &c., &c., &c....
of Our Special Grace have pardoned, remitted,
and released the said Daniel Peterson of and
from his said offence ... in testimony thereof
We have caused these Our Letters to be made
Patent and the Great Seal of Our Province to
be hereunto affixed ...

In the newspapers there had been talk of a general amnesty, but Dan had petitioned for a personal pardon. Not that he'd been so important. Poor old Mackenzie, sick and starving with his family in New York City, was still on the proscribed list, but one by one the other leaders were being pardoned. Smallfry like the Petersons usually came under blanket pardons, but feelings were still bitter even this long after, and Dan wanted to be on the safe side when he went back.

He didn't have to go back. He'd done well in the States—apprenticed to Matthew, learned the trade thoroughly. The only time he'd been tempted to cross the border was when they'd learned of their father's death.

A neighbour had sent word that he'd fallen from the ridgepole at a barn-raising. When Matthew had gone back to their old neighbourhood to arrange the funeral, another neighbour—one who'd always had a malicious tongue—had added that their father had been drunk at the time. Dan had felt both bitter and guilty when he'd heard that.

Whisky was provided by the barrel at barn-raisings, but his father had never touched it, had constantly pointed out to his sons the results of that weakness—wrecks who staggered from tavern to tavern while their families starved and their farms were reclaimed by the bush or the bank. No, if it were true only a sense of failure, of hopelessness, could have driven his father to drink. How much of that had been caused by the exile of his sons?

Matthew had tried, on one of his trips over the

border, to talk his father into coming to Buffalo to live with them but his father had turned his back, refused to listen despite the increasing hardships of working as a hired hand at his age. How Dan wished he had gone too! Surely between them they could have convinced him. But Matthew had insisted he could travel faster and safer alone.

Dan always wondered after that just how hard Matthew had tried. Out of his own sense of guilt had grown an undercurrent of annoyance with Matthew. Had Deborah been right that night at Crankshaw's? Did Matthew always take the easy way out? Several incidents over the years made him wonder if Matthew really felt strongly about the rebel cause, or if he was just in it for adventure. Certainly he pulled quickly out of any scheme that seemed doomed to failure. And one day, about a year after Dan's escape, he had turned his back on the exiles clustered in the border cities hatching plots, and instead thrown all his tremendous energy into building a carpentry business.

As they prospered Dan had learned every facet of the trade. He was grateful for that training, but growing in him was a need to be his own man, and a longing to return. At first he had not admitted even to himself what was drawing him back to Canada. But the day he'd told Matthew, said he needed to go home, he knew that he was going, not to Toronto, but to Queenston.

Now he was only minutes away. He'd been out

of the Lewiston Hotel at six that morning, had prowled the town restlessly for two hours while the freight was being loaded onto the ferry, and now, finally, was aboard. The early morning air had a strange crystal quality to it. Not a breath of wind rippled the surface of the green-blue Niagara. He could see himself mirrored in it, hatless, leaning over the railing in his new black frock coat, gazing across the six hundred yards of water that separated him from Queenston. Six years it had taken him to cross that tiny stretch again.

The first time it had been the early morning ferry as well, but the water then had been black and cold. He'd had butterflies in his stomach that time too. In Nat's clothes and one of Matthew's broad-brimmed hats he'd looked every inch the young apprentice. Matthew had introduced him to the captain and his two-man crew, had kept him chatting casually to the men loosing off the moorings. They'd been anxious enough to talk, to gossip about the soldiers who had arrived the previous day, about the way they were going to blast Mackenzie off his little island kingdom, about the crazy bee old Silas Hawkes had in his bonnet about the Wallbridges hiding a rebel.

"Ramrod Wallbridge," one of the sailors had guffawed. "The most stiff-backed officer in the local militia! Old Hawkes has gone right round the bend this time, God rot the greedy muckworm." And he had sent a mouthful of tobacco spittle arcing over the railing into the black water.

Dan had kept a smile nailed tightly to his face while his hands clenched and unclenched nervously in his jacket pockets. As the ferry steamed off he had caught sight of Ezekiel Crankshaw driving along the river road. The ferry had reached midstream, the boundary between Canada and the United States, when Dan saw Ezekiel wave his whip momentarily, perhaps in farewell, then crack it smartly to speed up the horse.

Dan could see the very spot where Ezekiel had raised his whip that grey December morning. Now it was lit by sunshine. Down the hillside, on the Queenston wharf, a crowd had started to collect—women with baskets over their arms, townsmen in frock coats, farmers in linsey-woolsey. He scanned the crowd intently, hoping. No one he knew. Wait a minute! Was that ferret-faced fellow...? No, it couldn't be. Silas Hawkes was long gone from Queenston, squeezed out by the silent disapproval of neighbours who had ceased to be customers. Hampered by the watchful eyes of sheriff and magistrate, he had sold his store, packed his wife and son onto the steamer and gone off to Montreal, or so Deborah had said in one of her letters.

Passengers crowded onto the ferry as departure time approached. With the toe of his boot, Dan nudged his satchel closer to his tool box. The handle settled down heavily on the fabric of the carpetbag, making bumps and hollows. One bump stuck up sharply. Dan smiled, thinking of that bundle of letters—twenty-four over the years. He had been afraid to write at first, afraid the American address might confirm the Hawkes' accusations, afraid they would think him presumptuous, afraid she wouldn't answer.

He had addressed the first one to her mother, a courtesy letter—as though a simple thank you could begin to be enough—and Deborah had added a long postscript to the answer. After that it had become a ritual to write on the fourth Sunday of one month and look for an answer the following month. He knew the letters were read out loud to the rest of the family. He'd never said anything that couldn't be shared, but he was hoping. He'd said in the last letter that he'd received a pardon and was coming home. There hadn't been time for her to answer the letter but he'd told her the day and the time. Of course, if she didn't come that didn't necessarily mean anything. After all, it wasn't market day and with spring planting to do they'd be busy, he told himself firmly. All the same, butterflies fluttered wildly in his stomach as the engine knocked and the ferry shuddered into life.

He couldn't bear to look again at the dock. Even at that distance he could have picked her out. He knew she wasn't there—yet. He looked instead at the Heights above the town where the monument to Brock, shattered by a rebel bomb three years before, pointed jaggedly at the sky. Dan felt as though the ghost of Brock frowned at him in stern disapproval for having run away. But you were fighting foreign enemies, not home-grown ones, Dan tried to excuse himself. He looked instead at the river road, following it with his eyes through the town and north to the spot where he and Deborah had crossed it that night. How intrepid she had been, how determined to let nothing stand in the way of what she felt she had to do.

He had never told her in his letters how often on a Sunday he had ridden from Buffalo to Lewiston to look across this stretch of water. Or how he had been tempted, the year she turned eighteen, to ask her to cross the river to him. But when he thought about what the Wallbridges had risked for him, he knew he couldn't ask them to send their only daughter to live in a foreign country on a labourer's wages. So even though, with each letter, he had feared to hear that she was about to be married to some local farmer's son, he had waited. Now that he could go to her a master carpenter and a free man, he was not afraid to ask. What he *was* afraid of—what none of her letters had even hinted at—was her answer. She had run so many risks for him that December six years ago, but...

In his imaginary walk he had reached the wooded escarpment where they had crouched that night. The rock outcropping with its lone pine was as visible as Brock's monument in the brilliant May sunshine. Could he have made it across from there? Some had made it across bigger gaps under worse conditions. But many, many others had been captured, some only minutes

from safety, to sicken and often die in freezing
jails, or to be transported to Van Diemen's Land
to toil under the jailer's lash, or in a few tragic
cases to be hanged. An icy shiver ran through
Dan. He had been one of the lucky ones in so
many ways. He closed his eyes momentarily, as
though to shut out the past, then deliberately
looked at the Queenston dock. He had so much to
be thankful for. Was it asking too much of Pro-
vidence to expect . . . ?

A wagon was clattering down the steep hill
that led into Queenston. Almost before the driver
pulled up, a girl leapt from it in a swirl of blue
skirts and came running along the pier to the
ferry wharf. A tall, glowing girl. Deborah.

He didn't hear the chatter around him or feel
the jostling crowd. He didn't feel the bump as the
ferry came alongside the dock or hear the rattle
as the gangplank was lowered. He just stood gazing down at her. She smiled back, her whole heart
in her shining eyes. He should have known that
in this, as in everything else, she wouldn't hold
back. She wouldn't make him wait for his answer.

* * *

Historical Note

In 1837 Upper Canada (Ontario) was a British Colony with a population drawn from many different backgrounds. The first settlers, who arrived in the 1780's, were fleeing from the United States, where a revolution had just thrown off British rule. These families, who had remained loyal to Britain when the Americans declared independence, were hunted out of the States by angry mobs and had to leave prosperous farms, businesses and good homes. Many, like Thad Wallbridge's parents, had to walk with all their possessions in packs on their backs through hostile Indian territory to reach refuge at Fort Niagara. When they reached their new land, Canada, they found it covered with dense forests. Although the British Government gave them land, tools to clear the land, and a year's supply of food, their new life was very harsh. Many of these Loyalists (as they were later called) never forgot how they had been treated in the United States, and they and their descendants were bitterly anti-American.

After 1800 other settlers came from the United States to Upper Canada. All the farmland in the Eastern United States had been settled, so many Americans came north to buy inexpensive Canadian land. Other Americans, like Silas Hawkes, were interested in making money by selling goods or services to the farmers. These people were not interested in politics, and lived in relative peace beside the Loyalists until the War of 1812 whipped up all the earlier anti-American feelings. After the war many British soldiers chose to stay in Canada. They were the third group of settlers.

Soldiers like Dan's father supported the Loyalist group in the colony, but many other immigrants were antagonistic to Britain. Ezekiel Crankshaw was typical of the hundreds of thousands of dispossessed Scots and Irish labourers who arrived in Upper Canada looking for a better life than they had had in Britain. With them came radical-thinking merchants, teachers and journalists such as William Lyon Mackenzie. These people knew that in Britain in 1832 all men (not just property owners, as before) had been given the right to vote, a say in how they were governed. They wanted the same laws to apply to Canada.

Canada, however, was divided into small colonies, each with its own Lieutenant-Governor sent out from Britain. He took his orders from the British Parliament, not the Canadian people. Although the colonists had the right to vote their own people into the Legislative Assembly, any laws passed by that body could be vetoed by the Legislative Council, whose members were chosen by the Lieutenant-Governor from the wealthy, land-owning families. Therefore, laws that would help farmers but might hurt rich landowners could be disallowed.

The farmers who cleared bush farms and had to sell their crops at market for a living had been angry for many years because wealthy people bought huge tracts of land and let them sit idle while they waited for the value to increase. This meant that roads needed to get crops to market were not improved, for these landowners did not bother to grade the roads that ran past their property. It also meant that bears and wolves had refuges from which to prey on the farmers' sheep and cattle. The burden of taxes was carried by the poorer farmers least able to pay them.

For over ten years Mackenzie attacked all these problems in his newspapers, *The Colonial Advocate* and *The Constitution*. He stood for office and was elected to the Legislative Assembly, where he attacked not only the laws but the people who made the laws, in such abusive language that he was three times thrown out of the Legislature (but three times re-elected by the people).

In 1836 two circumstances combined to bring all these grievances to a boil: a new Lieutenant-Governor, Sir Francis Bond Head, arrived from Britain, and the country suffered its most severe economic slump since the end of the War of 1812. 1836 was a bad year everywhere: Britain, Europe and the United States all felt the pinch. But in Upper Canada, where so many farmers were living on the edge of disaster, poor payment for their crops pushed them into bankruptcy. Like the Petersons, many lost their farms to the wealthy moneylenders who held the mortgages.

In addition, Sir Francis didn't understand the political situation. First he seemed willing to listen to the grievances voiced by moderate reformers (not radicals), then he announced that anyone voting for a reformer in the coming election would be considered a traitor to the Queen. In those days there was no secret ballot. The voter stood on a platform and shouted out the name of the person he was voting for. Unscrupulous candidates often hired bullies to beat up anyone who voted against them. Sir Francis seemed to be encouraging this kind of intimidation.

Even very moderate reformers were incensed enough to wonder whether Mackenzie was right when he said only a show of force could change the government's mind. By the autumn of 1837 people were so enraged by the situation that Mackenzie thought he had enough backing to stage a rebellion.

Unfortunately, Mackenzie was a better public speaker than he was a military commander, and he did not have complete control over his lieutenants. While he sent couriers to tell the farmers in one section of the country to meet at Montgomery's Tavern north of Toronto on December 7th, one of his lieutenants sent couriers telling others to come on the 4th. No one thought to make provision for feeding the hundreds of men who began to gather. Anthony Van Egmond, his chief military adviser and a former officer in the Napoleonic Wars, tried to impose some military discipline on the groups that arrived, but few had been soldiers and even fewer had proper weapons. Some had muskets or rifles; most were armed with pitchforks or pikes. They had no chance at all against the government forces with small cannon, muskets, rifles and a militia that included many former army men. Within minutes the rebels had been routed.

The real tragedy came later. In rounding up the rebels Sir Francis was vindictive. Houses were burned, women and children turned out into the snow, men herded into freezing, filthy, crowded jails to await sentencing. Although many minor participants were sent home within a few days, anyone thought to be a leader was held without trial for weeks, sometimes months.

The hundreds of rebels who escaped to the States continued the fight from bases in border cities. Sympathetic Americans rallied around Mackenzie and his rebels on Navy Island, planning to strike at Canada from there. Although they were soon forced to abandon Navy Island, they tried on three occasions to invade Canada from other bases. All three attempts failed, leading only to more hangings and more transportations to Van Diemen's Land, where Britain maintained a prison colony.

However, the rebellion was not a complete failure. It showed the British Government that something had to be done. They sent Lord Durham to investigate the situation and propose remedies. He was willing to listen to the moderate reformers. By 1848 Upper and Lower Canada had been joined to form one colony, and had been granted the right to elect representatives from their own populations to make and administer all their domestic laws.

One of the first things the local councils did was to tax the wild land so heavily that many speculators were forced to sell. This gave farmers who would clear and cultivate the land a chance to buy it. As a result, many of the problems faced earlier by small farmers, problems that led people like Daniel and Matthew Peterson into the rebellion, were improved in the years following it.

During those years more and more of the rebels were pardoned, but Mackenzie himself, living in poverty and despair with his family in New York City, remained outlawed. Finally, in 1849, even he was pardoned. In 1850 he brought his family back to Toronto, where his well-wishers bought him a small house, 82 Bond Street, now restored as a museum.

Barbara Greenwood

As a child, the stories Barbara Greenwood read were all set in the past. Through the magic of books, she followed the Oregon Trail, was captured by Indians, travelled in gypsy wagons, built railroads and lived in an English castle.

Later, Barbara took an interest in Canada's rich and colourful past, and found herself focusing on pioneers. Volunteer work at a museum where she dressed in an 1850s costume helped her to create the perfect setting for *A Question of Loyalty*.

Barbara currently works as a writer and creative writing teacher. She is a frequent speaker at conferences and a past-president of CANSCAIP, a dynamic group devoted to promoting children's literature throughout Canada. Barbara was awarded the 1982 Vicky Metcalf Award for "A Major Resolution." Her other books include *Spy in the Shadows* (Kids Can Press), *Her Special Vision: A Biography of Jean Little* (Irwin), *Jeanne Sauvé* (Fitzhenry & Whiteside) and *Klondike Challenge: Rachel Hanna, Frontier Nurse* (Grolier).